SECOND EDITION

Volume II

THE REAL B♭ BOOK

ISBN 0-634-06077-5

HAL•LEONARD® CORPORATION

7777 W. BLUEMOUND RD. P.O. BOX 13819 MILWAUKEE, WI 53213

Visit Hal Leonard Online at
www.halleonard.com

PREFACE

The B♭ Real Book is the answer to the fake book. It is an alternative to the plethora of poorly designed, illegible, inaccurate, badly edited volumes which abound on the market today. The B♭ Real Book is extremely accurate, neat, and is designed, above all, for practical use. This edition offers the horn player the luxury of on-the-spot sight reading without having to transpose. Every effort has been made to make it enjoyable to play. Here are some of the primary features:

1. FORMAT
    a. The book is professionally copied and meticulously checked for accuracy in melody, harmony, and rhythms.
    b. Form within each tune, including both phrases and larger sections, is clearly delineated and placed in obvious visual arrangement.
    c. All two-page tunes open to face one another.
    d. Most standard-type tunes remain true to their original harmonies with little or no reharmonization. The exceptions include a handful of jazz interpretations of popular songs and Broadway showtunes, as well as some modifications using modern notation and variation among turnarounds.

2. SELECTION OF TUNES AND EDITING
    a. Major jazz composers of the last 60 years are highlighted, with special attention given to the 1960s and 1970s.
    b. While some commonly played tunes are absent from the book, many of the classics are here, including bop standards and a fine selection of Duke Ellington masterpieces. See Real Book volumes 1 and 3 for more tunes.
    c. Many of the included arrangements represent the work of the jazz giants of the last 40 years – Miles, Coltrane, Shorter, Hancock, Rollins, Silver, and Monk, as well as a variety of newer artists.
    d. A variety of recordings and alternate editions were consulted to create the most accurate and user-friendly representations of the tunes, whether used in a combo setting or as a solo artist.

3. SOURCE REFERENCE
    a. The composer(s) of every tune is listed.
    b. Every song presented in the Real Book is now fully licensed for use.

Second Edition

This new edition contains tunes that are re-arranged, re-transcribed and most importantly, licensed, so that you may study and play these works more accurately and legally. Enjoy!

W

Y

REPEAT HEAD IN/OUT

14

ALFIE'S THEME

— Sonny Rollins

(SWING)

(Ballad) ALL ALONE (LEFT ALONE)

—Billie Holiday/Mal Waldron

(All Of A Sudden) My Heart Sings

(Med. Ballad)
(Even 8ths)

— Harold Rome / Jamblan / Laurent Herpin

ALTO ITIS

—OLIVER E. NELSON

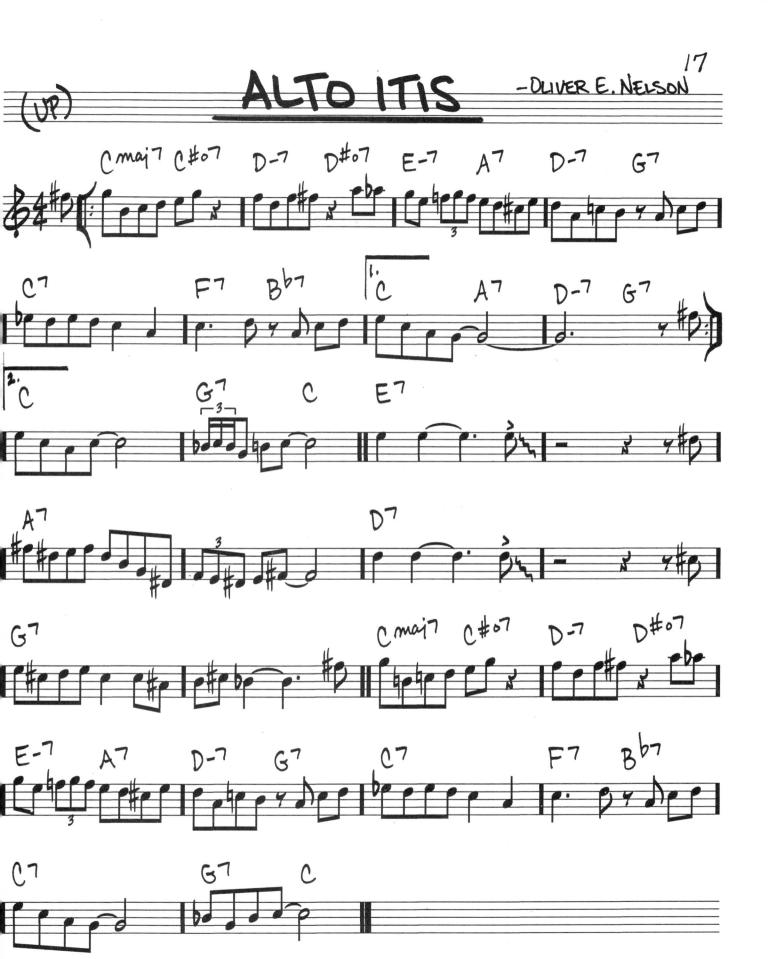

Another Star

– Stevie Wonder

20 APRIL SKIES
-Buddy Collette

(MED. UP)

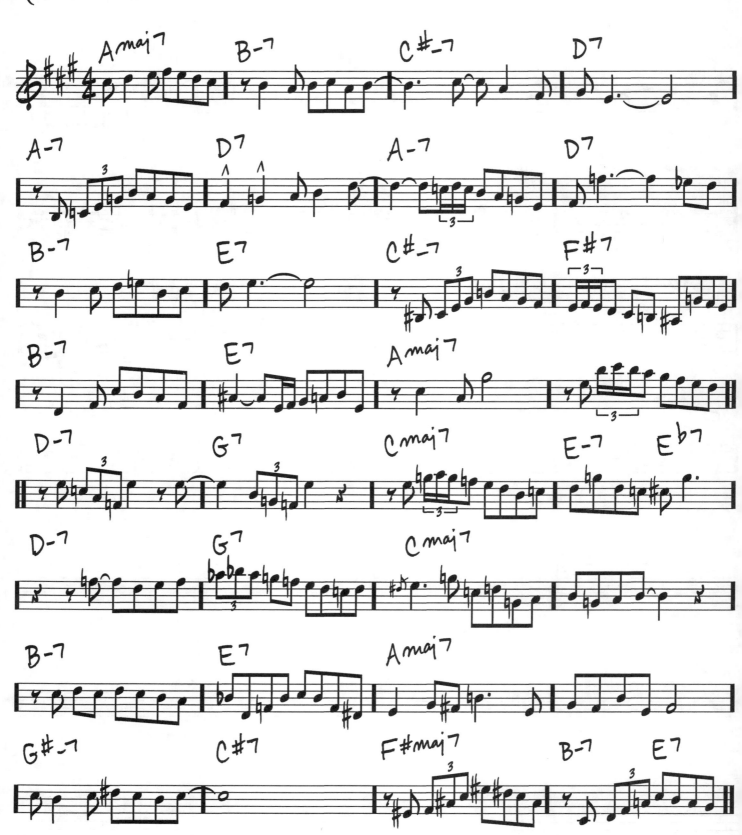

AFTER SOLOS, D.C. AL⊕

ASK ME NOW

—Thelonious Monk

(Walking Ballad)

AZURE

-Duke Ellington

(MED SLOW SWING)

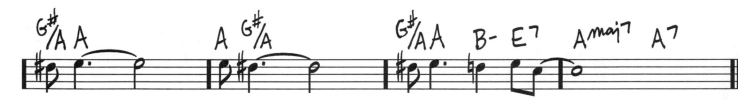

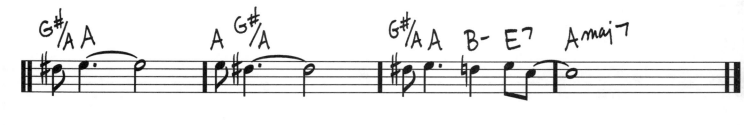

BA-LUE BOLIVAR BA-LUES-ARE
(BOLIVAR BLUES)

(MED. BLUES)

—Thelonious Monk

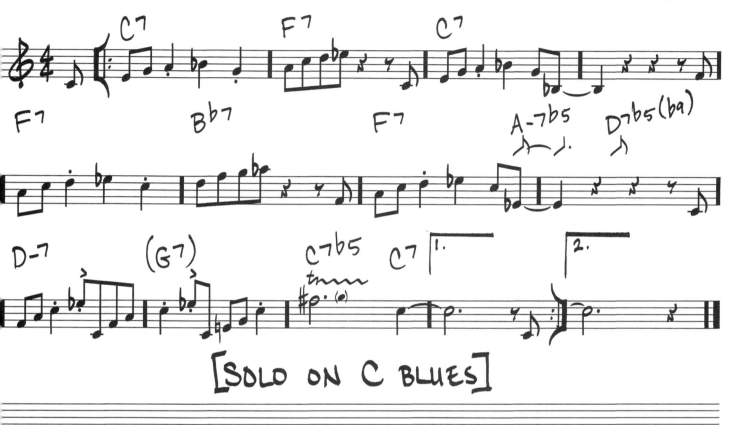

[SOLO ON C BLUES]

BABY, IT'S COLD OUTSIDE

(MED.)

28

—FRANK LOESSER

CAN ALSO BE PLAYED "CALL AND RESPONSE"
STYLE WITH ADDITIONAL MELODY INSTRUMENT

BAGS AND TRANE

—Milt Jackson

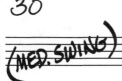

BAGS' GROOVE

—Milt Jackson

A BALLAD

32
(SLOW)

—GERRY MULLIGAN

BALTIMORE ORIOLE

— Hoagy Carmichael
— Paul Francis Webster

(MED. BALLAD)

BARBADOS

—Charlie Parker

(FAST BOP)

BARBARA

-Horace Silver

(JAZZ WALTZ)

BASIN STREET BLUES

-Spencer Williams

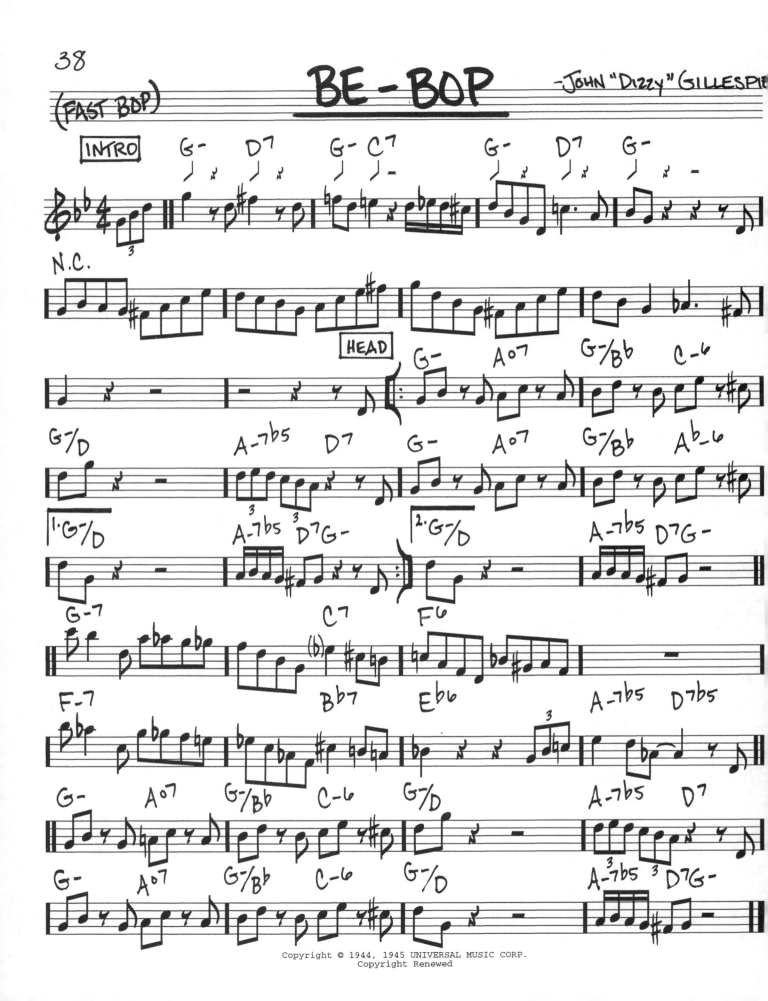

BETTER LEAVE IT ALONE

- Clifford Jordon

(MED.)

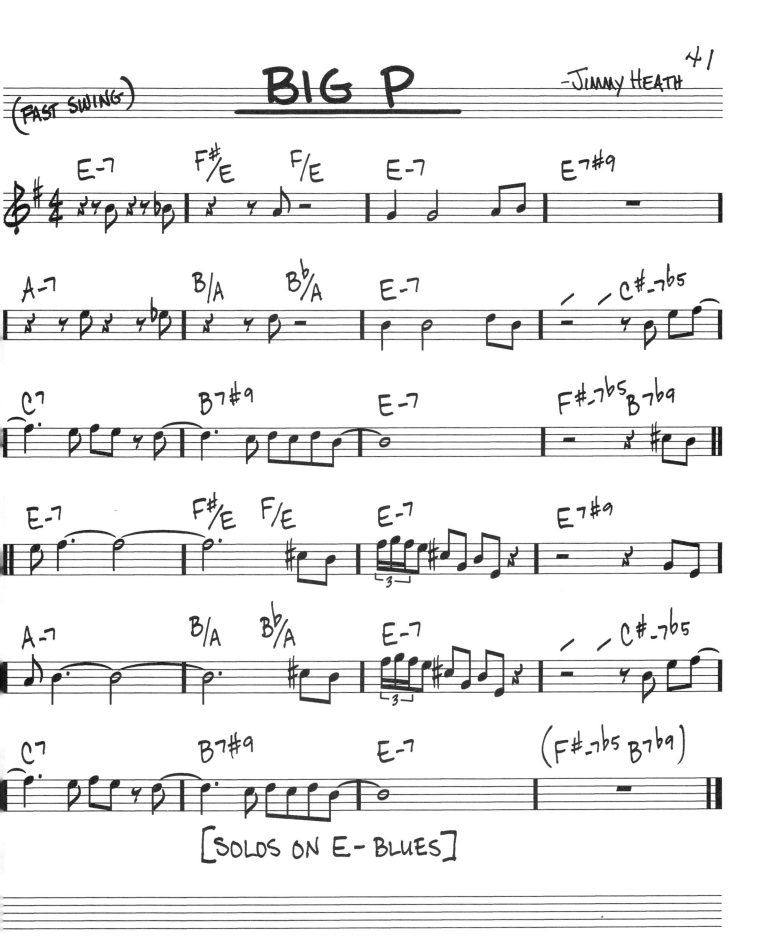

[SOLOS ON E- BLUES]

BILLIE'S BLUES
(I LOVE MY MAN)
—Billie Holiday

(SLOW BLUES)

AFTER SOLOS, D.C. AL ⊕
(TAKE 2nd ENDING)

BILLIE'S BOUNCE
(BILL'S BOUNCE)

~ Charlie Parker

(FAST BLUES)

AFTER SOLOS, D.C. AL ⊕
(TAKE REPEAT)

BIRD FEATHERS

-Charlie Parker

(BOP)

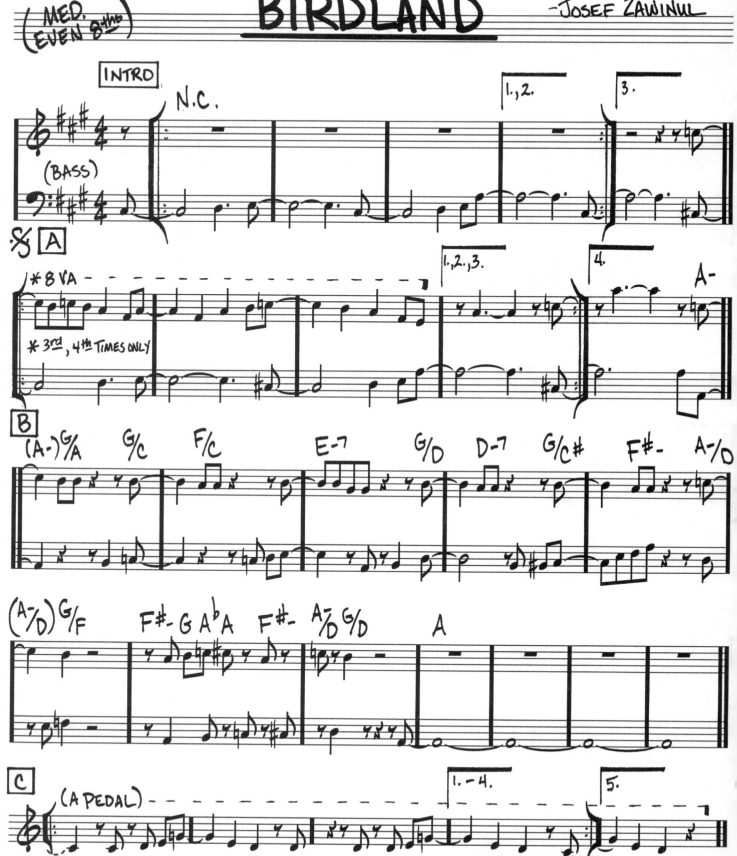

BIRDLAND

—Josef Zawinul

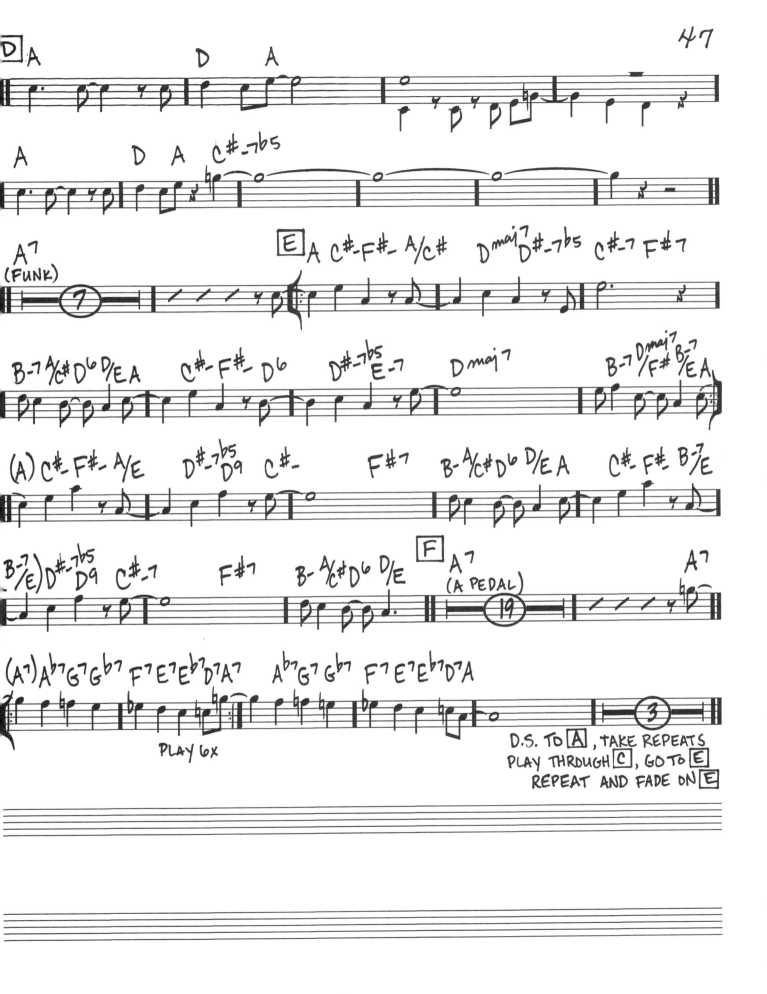

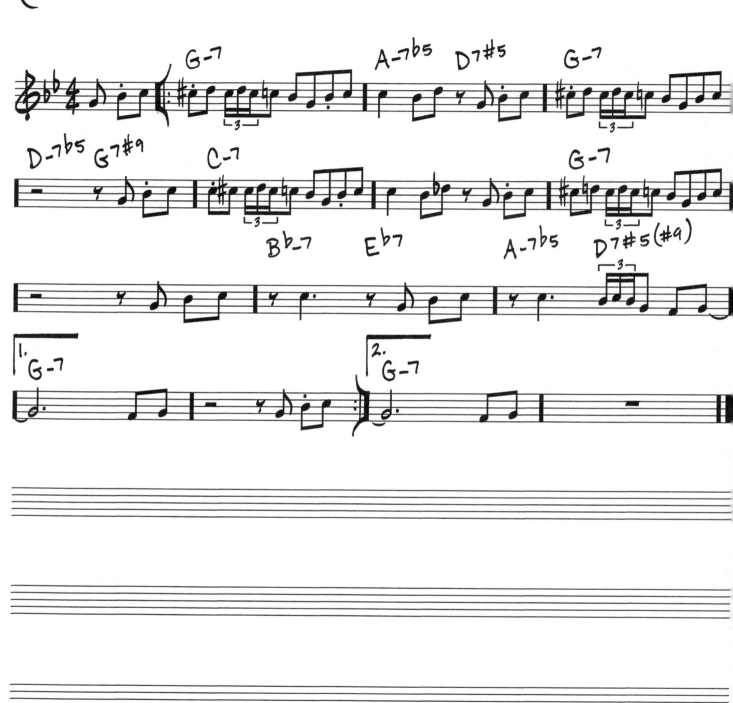

Birk's Works

48

(MED. SWING)

—Dizzy Gillespie

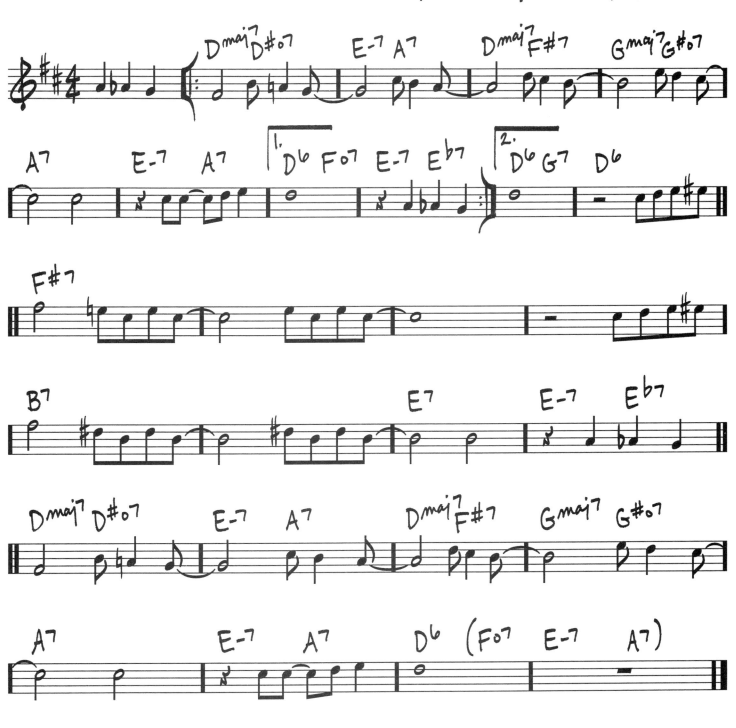

Black And Tan Fantasy

- Duke Ellington / Bub Miley

SOLO OVER C BLUES

AFTER SOLOS, D.C. AL ⊕

RIT. - - - - -

Blame It On My Youth
(Ballad)

-Oscar Levant/Edward Heyman

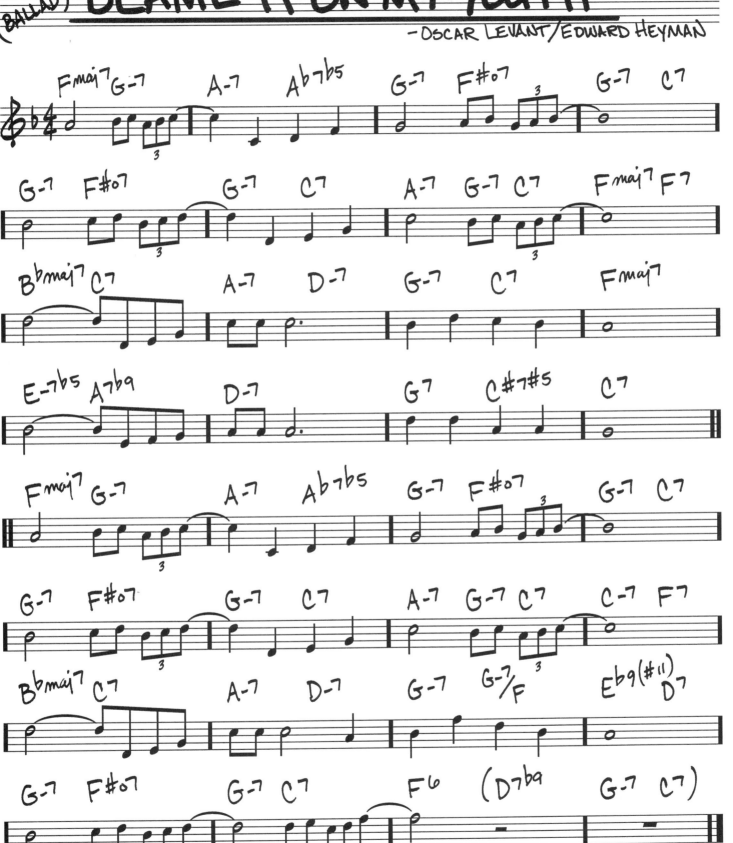

BLOOMDIDO

-CHARLIE PARKER

(Fast Blues)

BLOW MR. DEXTER

(MED. UP BLUES) —Dexter Gordon

BLUE SERGE

— Mercer Ellington

(SLOW BLUES)

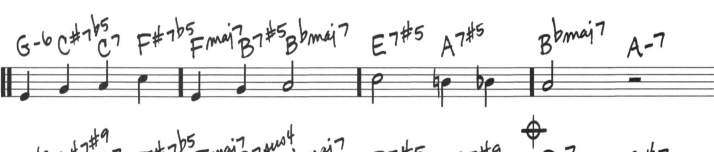

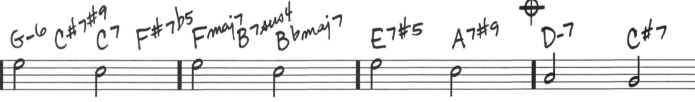

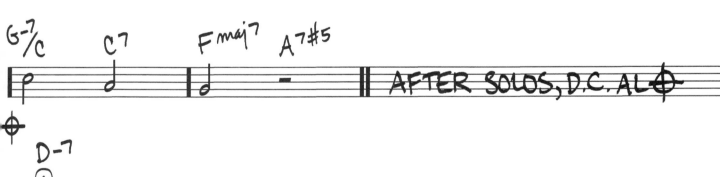

AFTER SOLOS, D.C. AL ⊕

56

BLUE SEVEN

—Sonny Rollins

(MED. BLUES)

BLUE SILVER
-Horace Silver

(MED.)

BLUES BY FIVE
—RED GARLAND

(MED. FAST)

60

(MED FAST)

BLUES FOR WOOD

— Woody Shaw

(G-7 ON BEAT 1 FOR SOLOS)

Blues in the Closet

(BRIGHT BLUES)

-Oscar Pettiford

BLUES MARCH

—BENNY GOLSON

(MED.)

AFTER SOLOS, D.C. AL ⊕
(TAKE REPEAT)

BOHEMIA AFTER DARK

(MED. FAST)

-Oscar Pettiford

BOOKER'S WALTZ

-Booker Little

(JAZZ WALTZ)

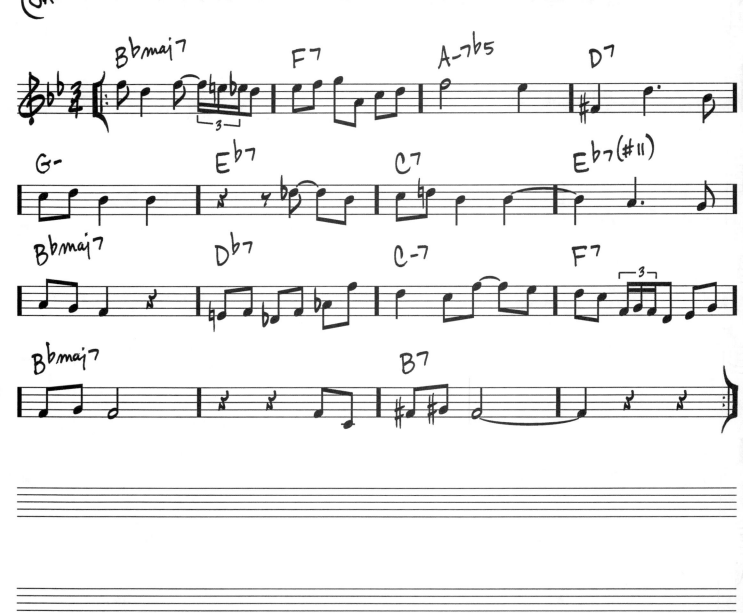

BRIAN'S SONG

-Michel Legrand

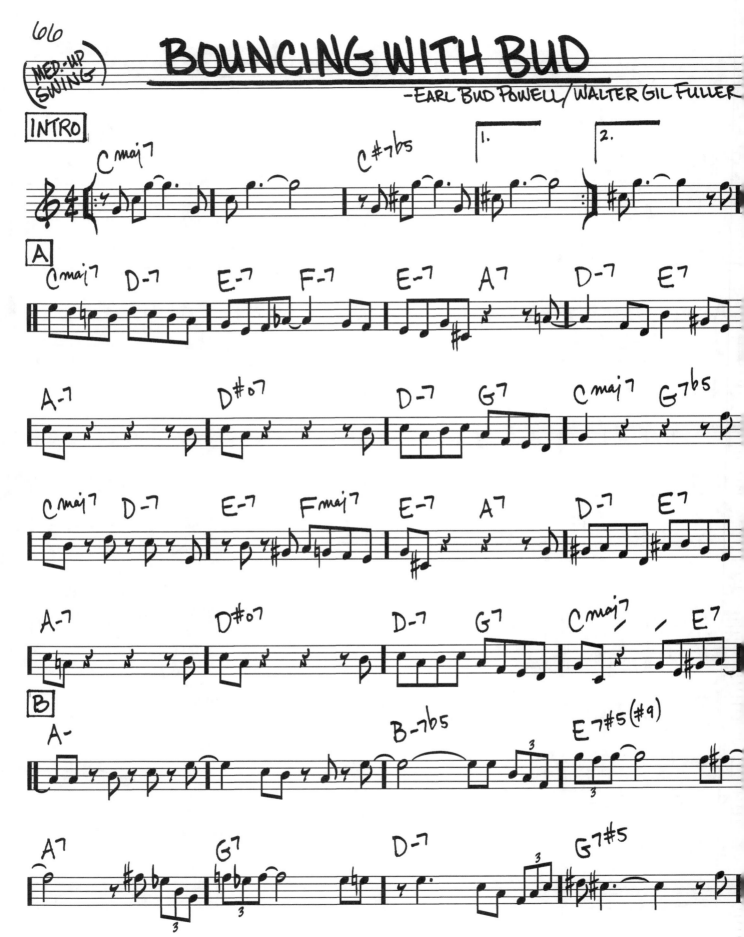

BRIGHT BOY

-John Bright

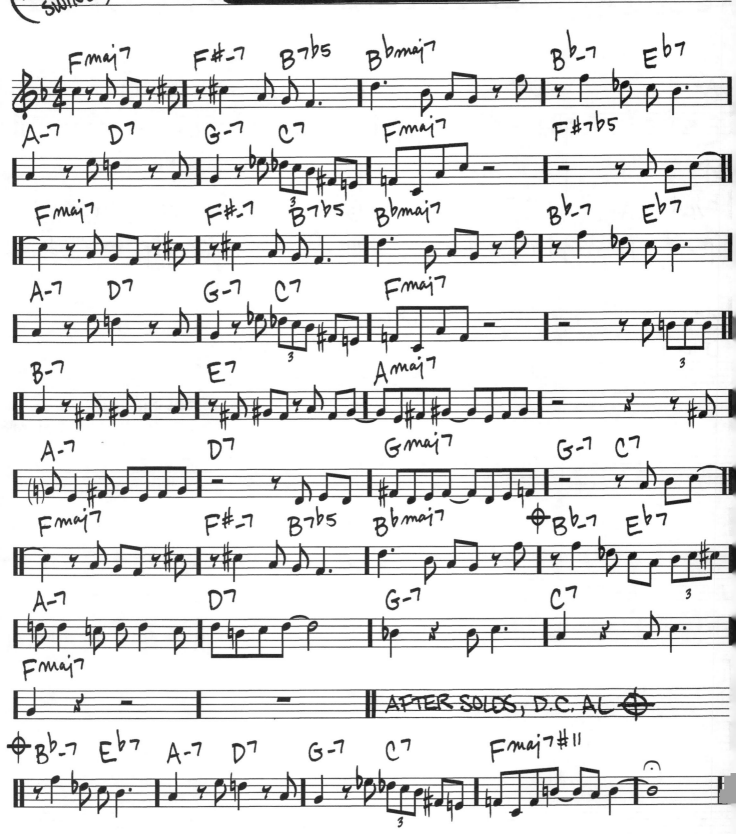

BRILLIANT CORNERS

—Thelonious Monk

1st TIME: SLOW WALK, EVEN 8ths
ON REPEAT: MED.-UP SWING

REPEAT MELODY DOUBLE-TIME SWING   FINE
SOLOS FOLLOW SAME FORMAT

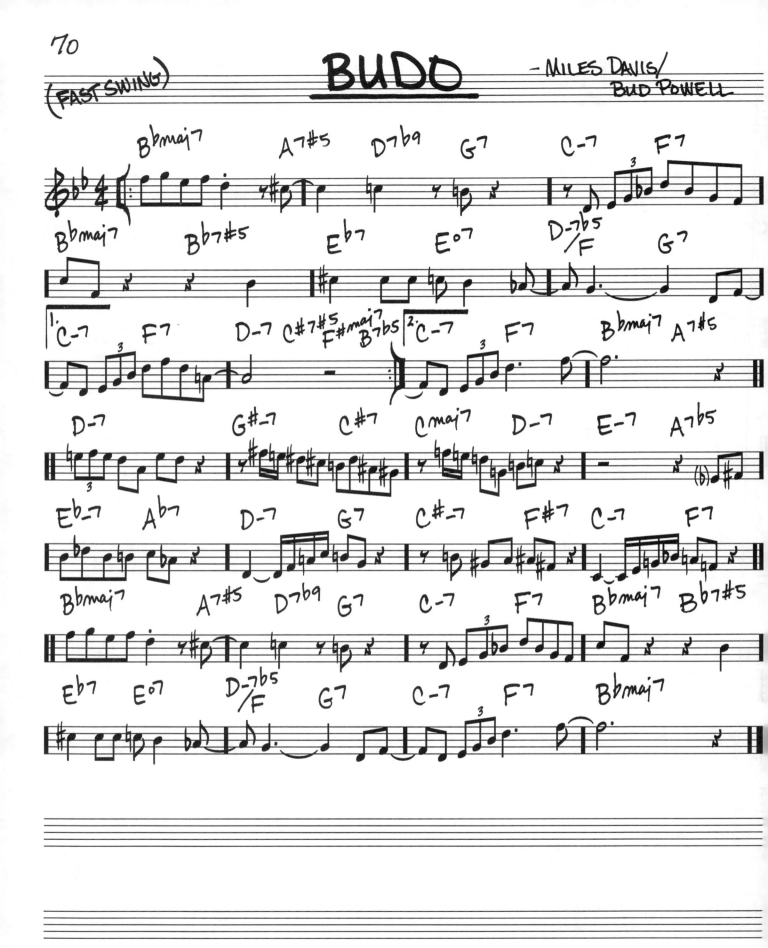

BUNKO

-Lennie Niehaus

BUSTER RIDES AGAIN

-Earl "Bud" Powell

BYE BYE BLACKBIRD
-Ray Henderson/
Mort Dixon

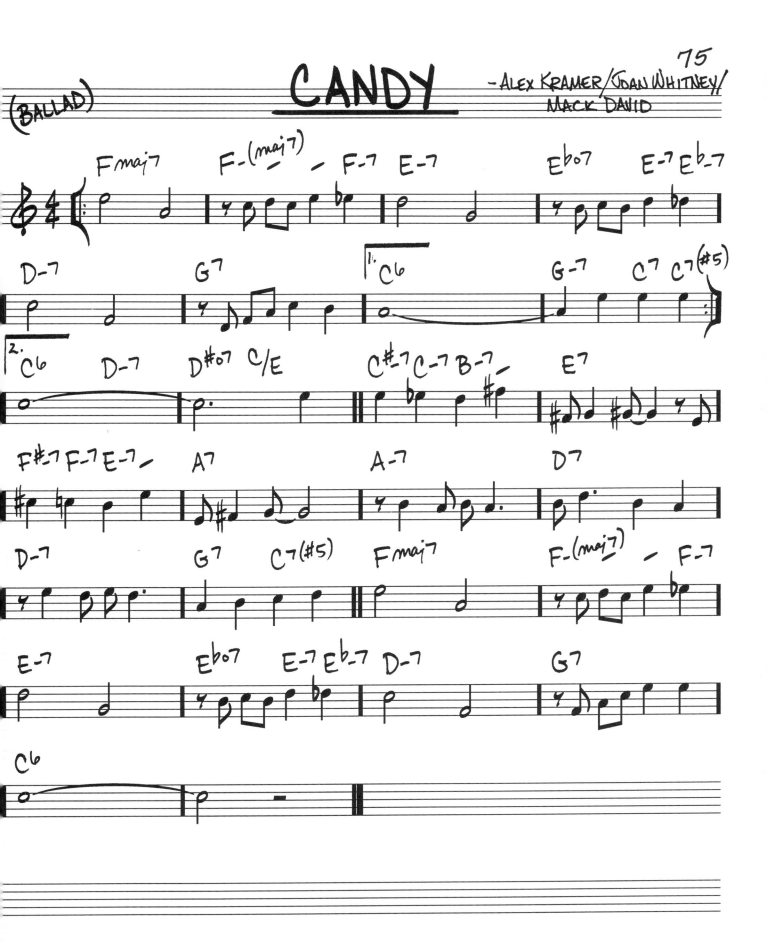

CANTELOPE ISLAND
— Herbie Hancock

76
(MED. JAZZ)
FUNK

INTRO

G-7 (MELODY)

HEAD

G-7

RHYTHM CONT. SIM.

Eb7

E-11

G-7
(INTRO VAMP)

REPEAT HEAD IN
AFTER SOLOS, PLAY HEAD ONCE
VAMP INTRO TIL FADE

Cast Your Fate to the Wind

~Vince Guaraldi/Carel Werber

(MED.)

CHAMELEON

(MED. FUNK)

— Herbie Hancock / Paul Jackson /
Harvey Mason / Bennie Maupin

THE CHAMP
—Dizzy Gillespie

80

* BASS WALKS IMPLIED CHANGES

FINE

[SOLOS ON B♭ BLUES]

ON CUE BETWEEN SOLOS:

BETWEEN SOLOS

LAST TIME (BEFORE HEAD OUT)

NEXT SOLO BEGINS

D.S. AL FINE
(TAKE REPEAT)

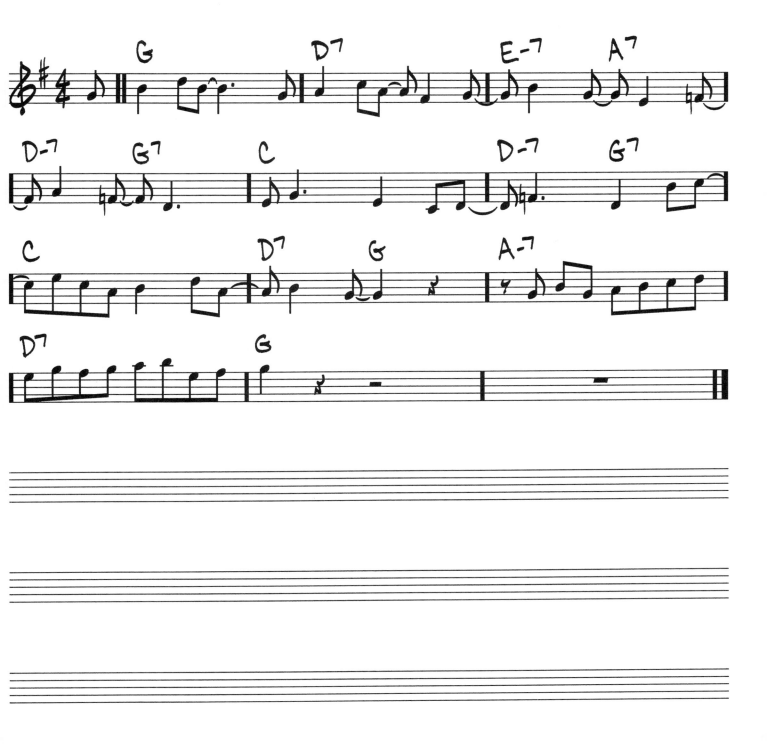

CHEESECAKE

-- Dexter Gordon

CIRCLE

84

— Miles Davis

(MED. JAZZ WALTZ)

COMIN' HOME BABY

-Bob Dorough/ Ben Tucker

(SOUL JAZZ)

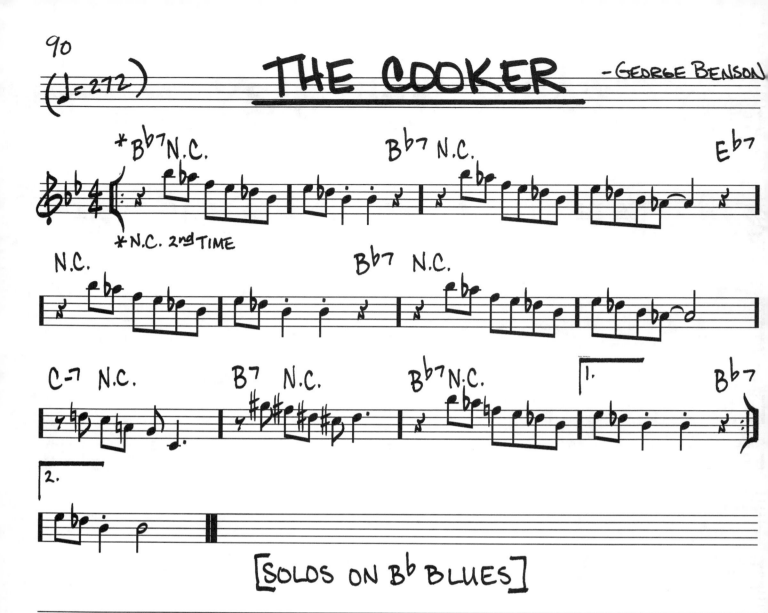

[SOLOS ON Bb BLUES]

Cool Blues

— Charlie Parker

(BRIGHT BLUES)

THE CORE

— Freddie Hubbard

(MED. SWING)

COUSIN MARY

-John Coltrane

REPEAT HEAD IN/OUT

CRAZEOLOGY

—Bennie Harris

(BOP)

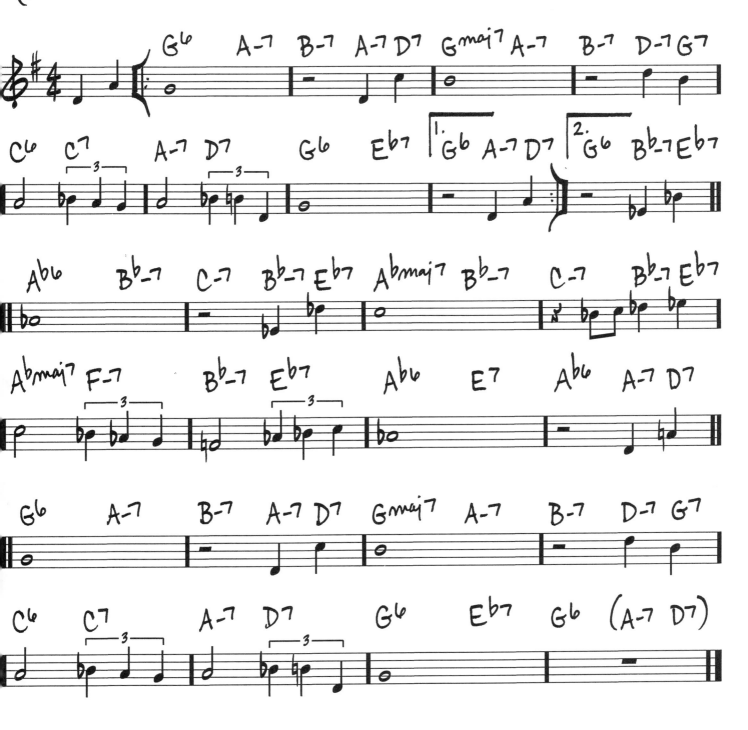

CRISS CROSS

-Thelonious Monk

(MED. SWING)

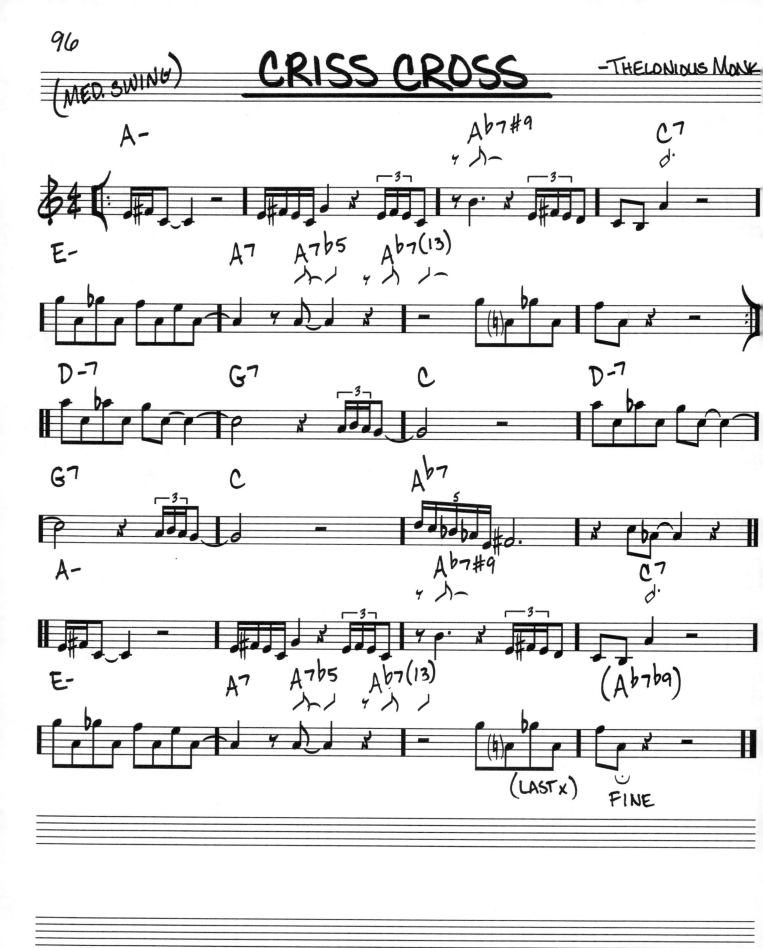

CROSSCURRENT

-Lennie Tristano

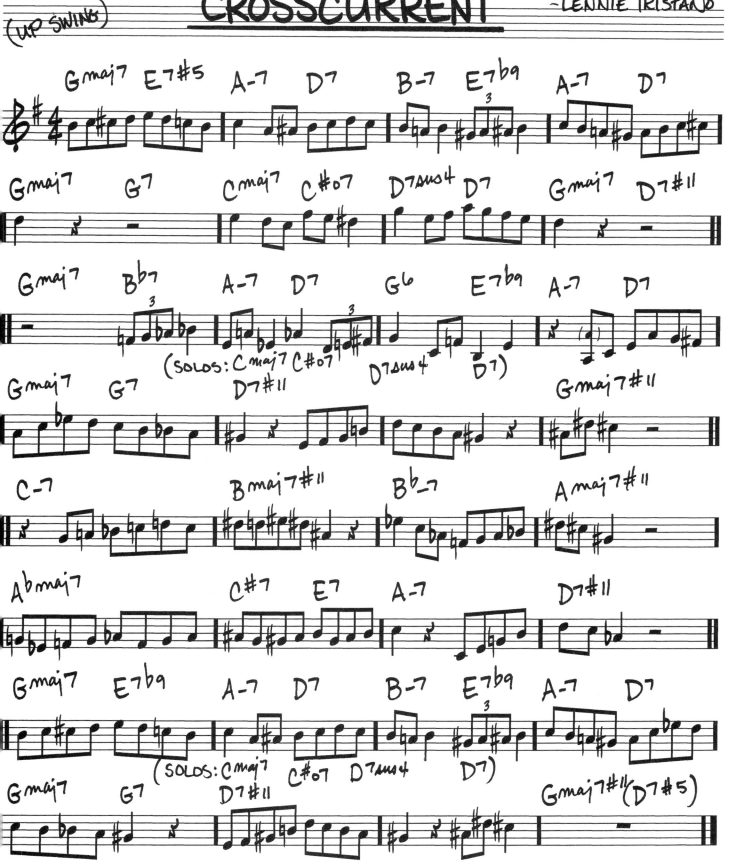

DAT DERE

-Bobby Timmons

(MED. SWING)

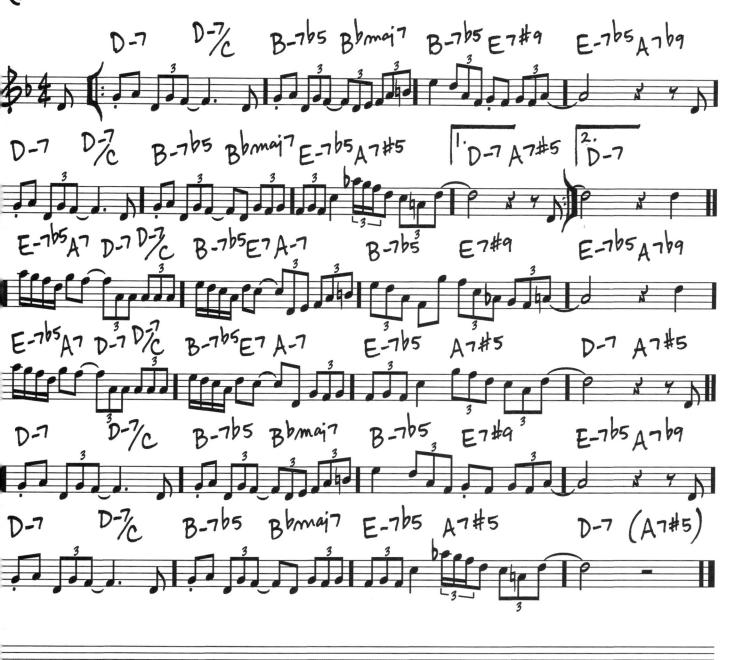

100

DEWEY SQUARE
-Charlie Parker

DEXTER RIDES AGAIN

-Dexter Gordon/Earl "Bud" Powell

(MED.)

DINDI

DO I LOVE YOU BECAUSE YOU'RE BEAUTIFUL?

(MED.)

-Richard Rodgers/Oscar Hammerstein II

DO NOTHIN' TILL YOU HEAR FROM ME

-Duke Ellington/Bob Russell

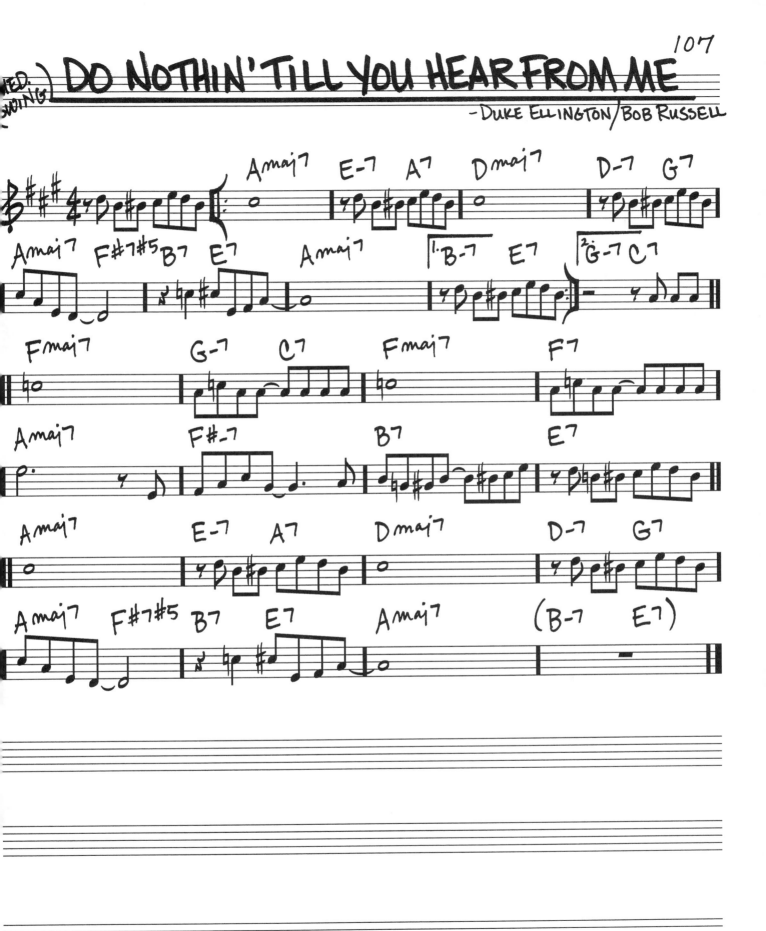

Do You Know What It Means to Miss New Orleans

-- Eddie De Lange / Louis Alter

(Slow Swing)

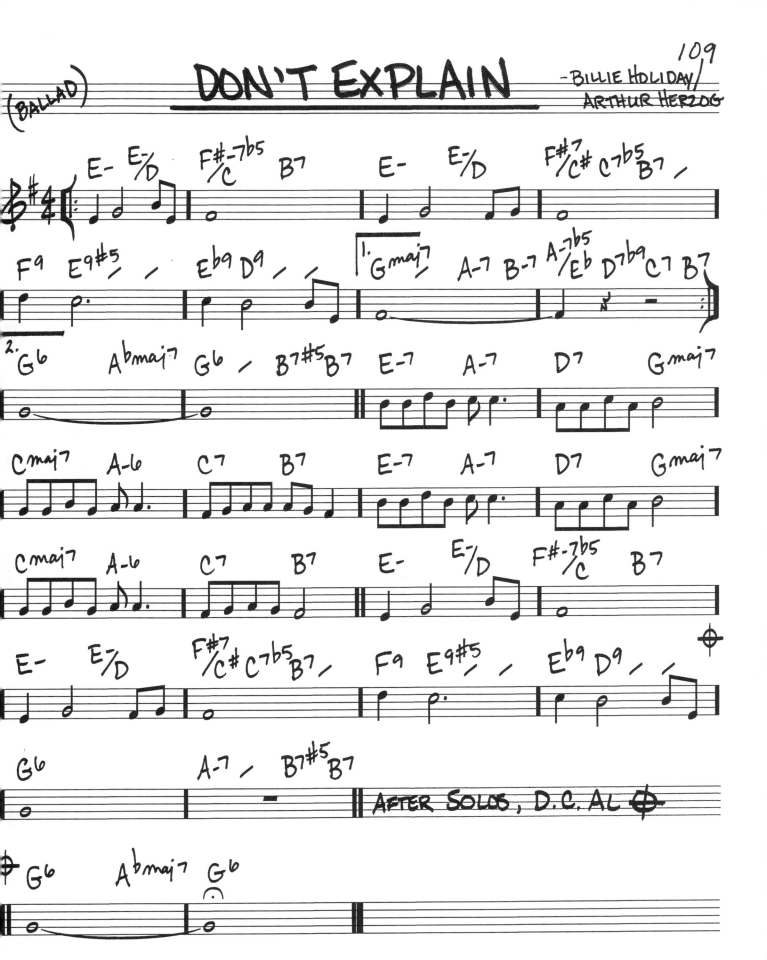

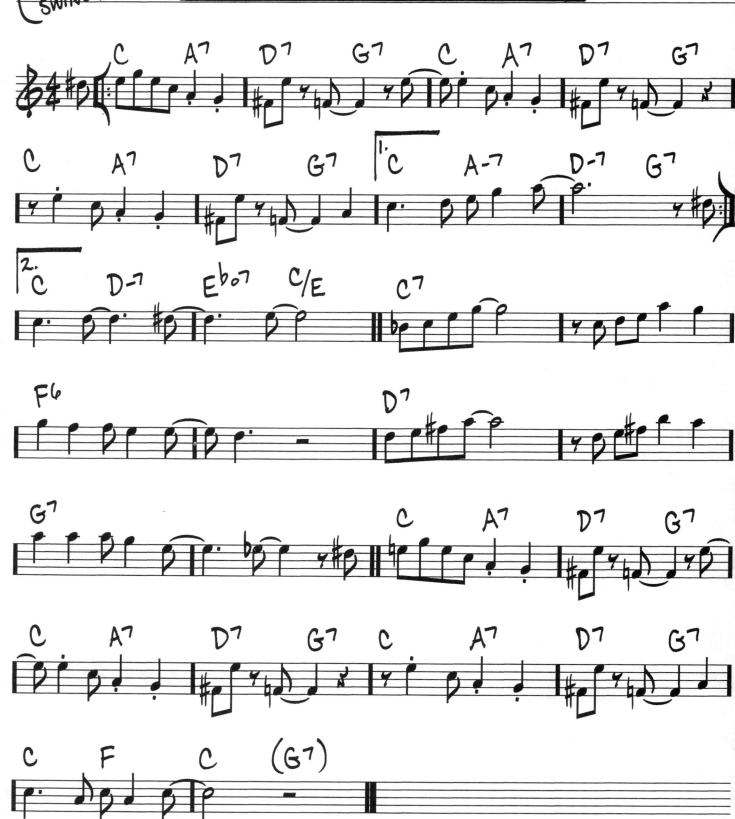

110

DOWN FOR DOUBLE — Fred Greene

(MED. UP SWING)

DOXY

— Sonny Rollins

(MED.)

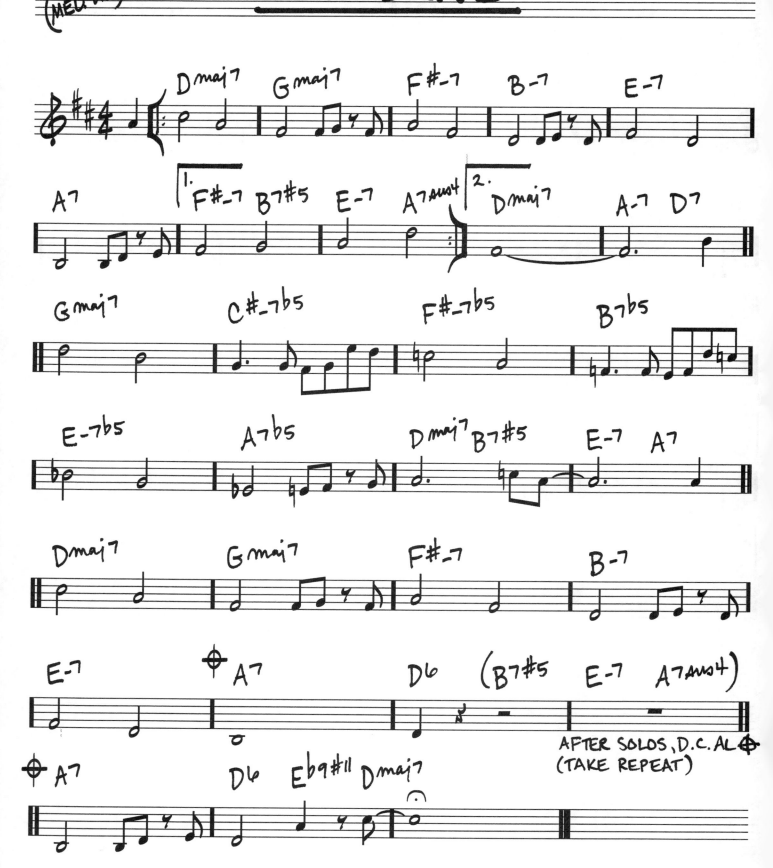

Duff

-Hampton Hawes

ECLYPSO

~Tommy Flanagan

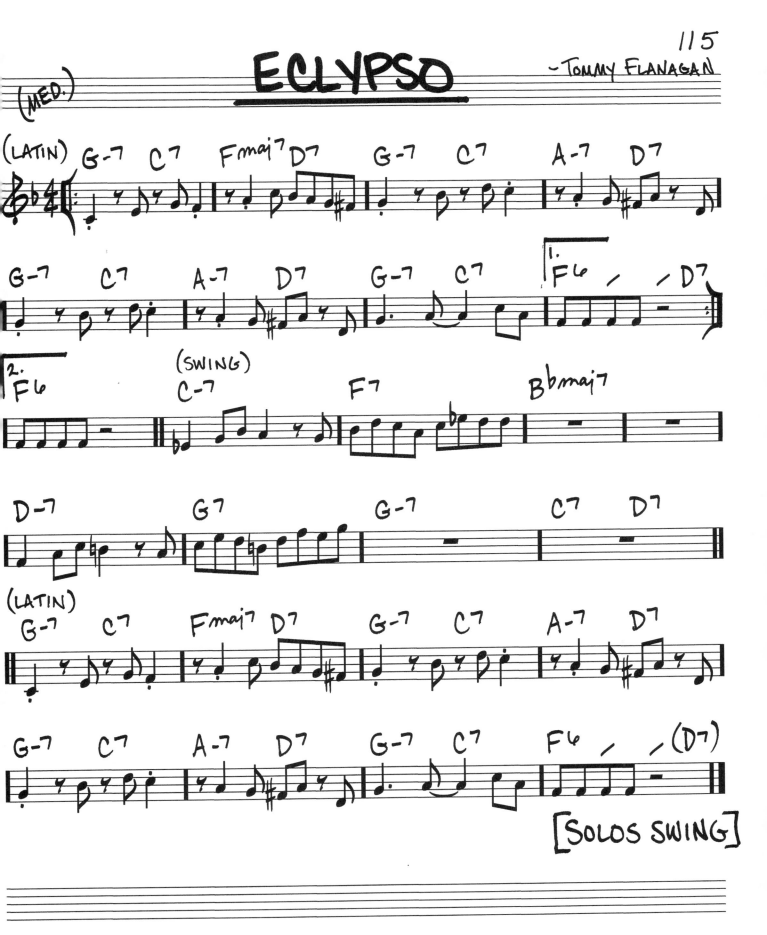

[SOLOS SWING]

116

(MED. UPSWING) **EINBAHNSTRASSE** —RON CARTER

ELORA

-J.J. Johnson

EPILOGUE

-Bill Evans

ESTATE

—Bruno Martino/ Bruno Brighetti

(MED. BOSSA)

AFTER SOLOS, D.C. AL ⊕

[SOLOS ON G-BLUES]

124

EZZ-THETIC

-George Russell

(MED UP)

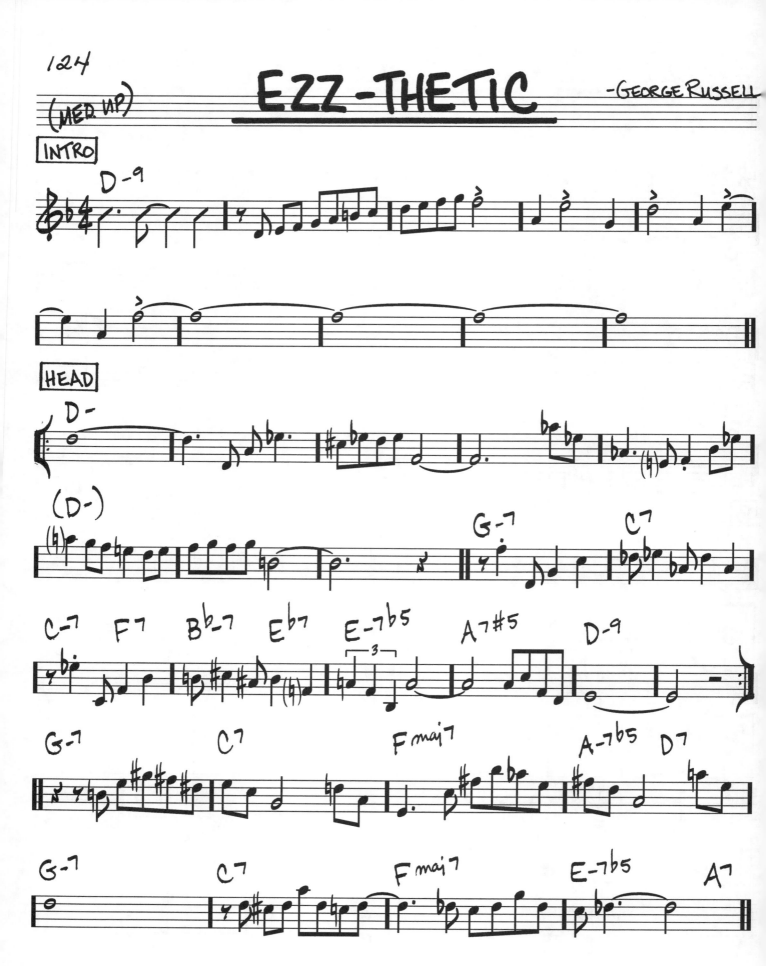

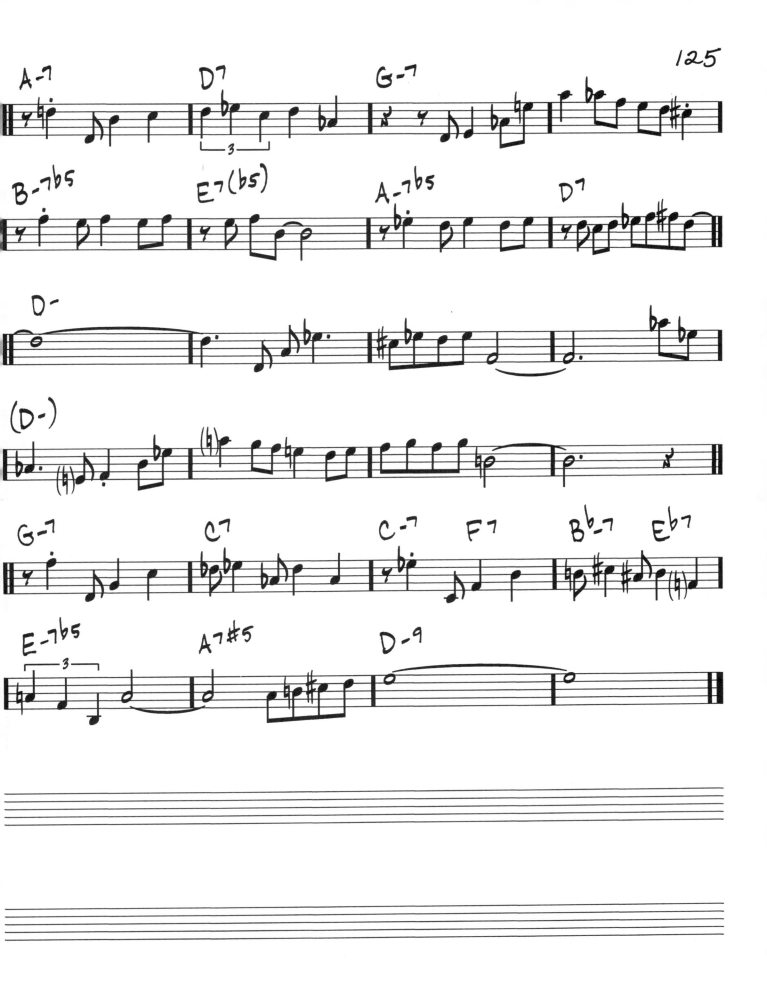

Feels So Good

— Chuck Mangione

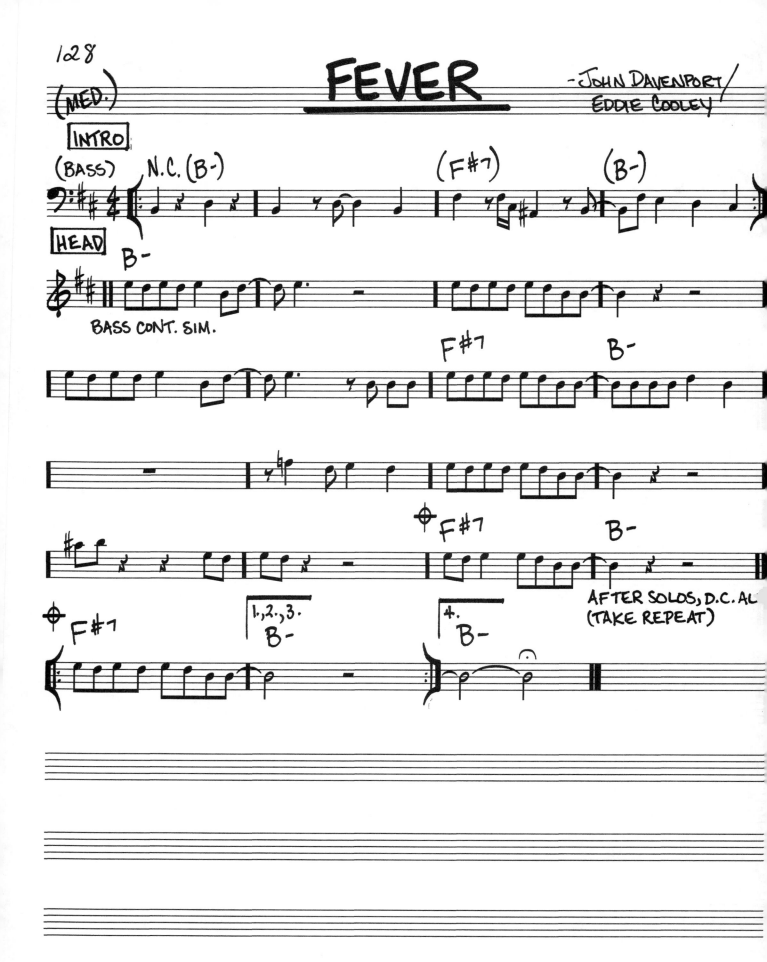

52ⁿᵈ STREET THEME

-Thelonious Monk

(UP)

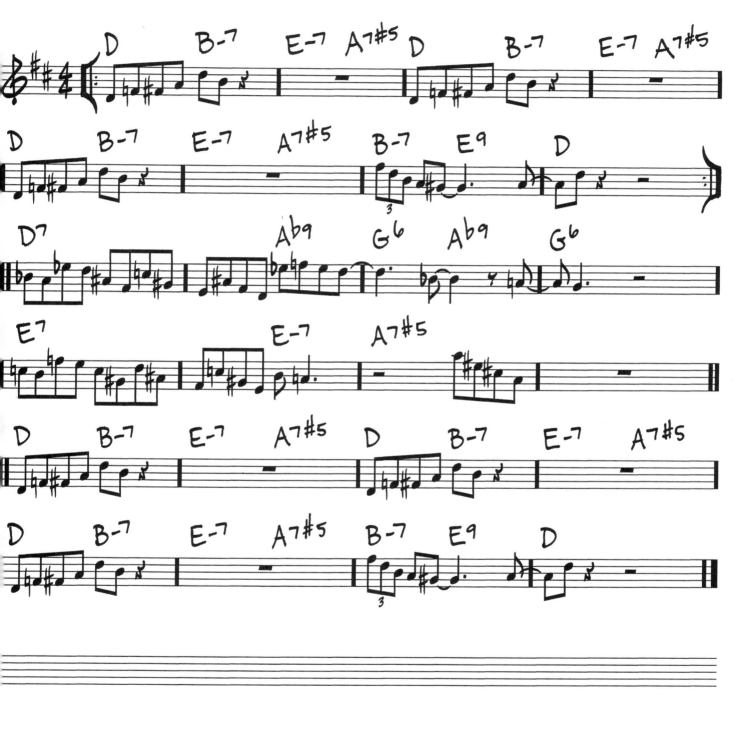

First Trip

— Ron Carter

(Med.)

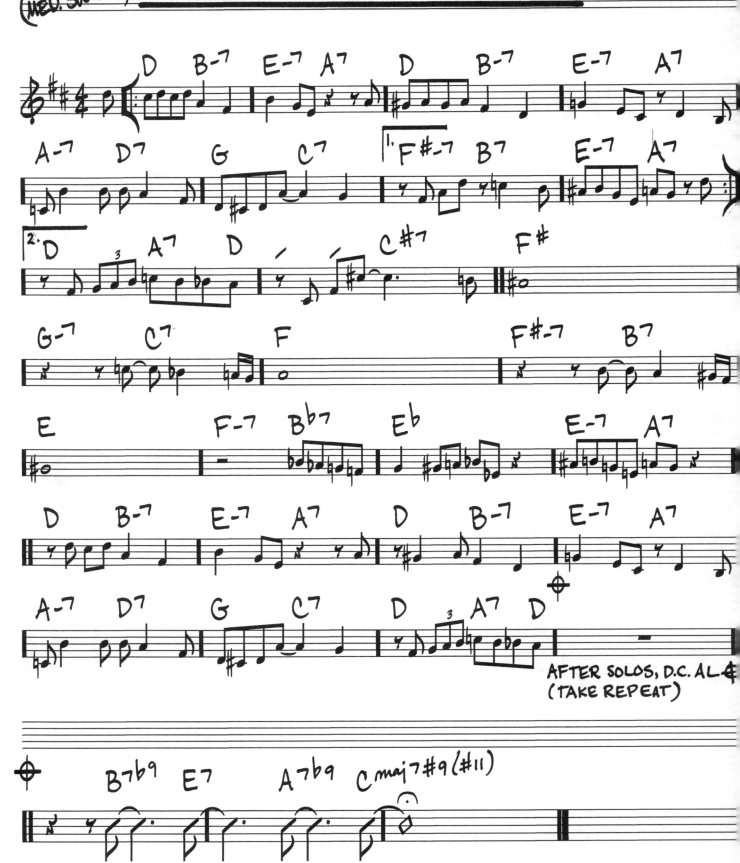

FIVE BROTHERS

132

(MED. SWING)

-Gerry Mulligan

FIVE SPOT AFTER DARK

- BENNY GOLSON

(MED.)

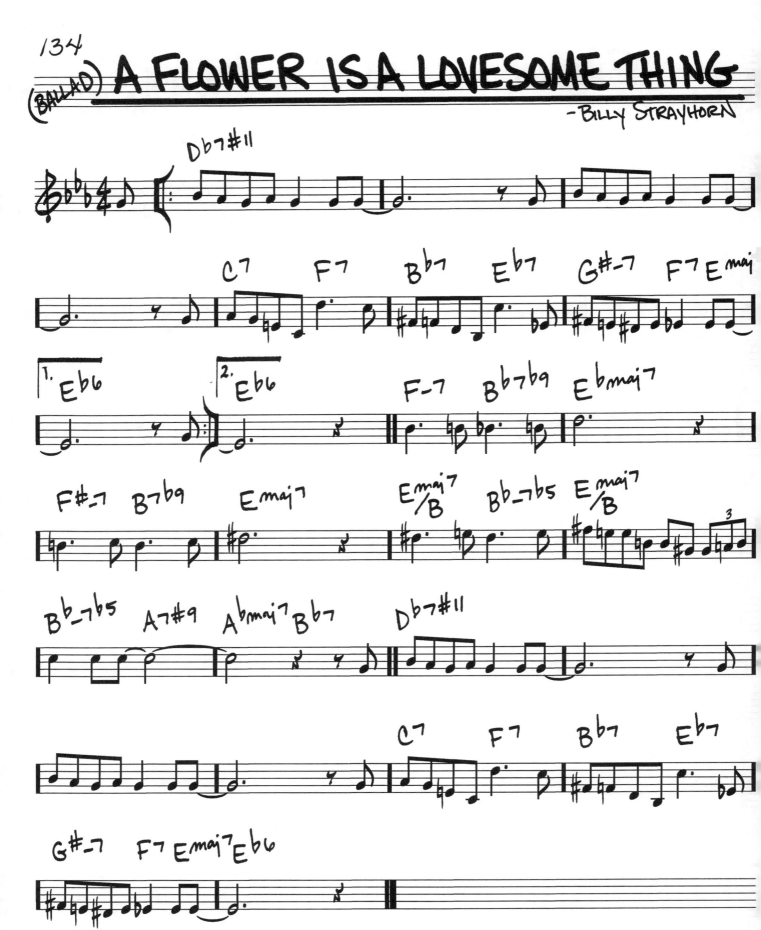

134

(Ballad) A FLOWER IS A LOVESOME THING

– Billy Strayhorn

Fly Me to the Moon
(In Other Words)

-Bart Howard

THE FOLKS WHO LIVE ON THE HILL

(BALLAD)

-Jerome Kern/Oscar Hammerstein II

138

Four Brothers
— Jimmy Giuffre

(MED. UP SWING)

FREIGHT TRANE

—Tommy Flanagan

(MED. UP)

TAKE 1ST ENDING ON SOLOS

Fox Hunt

-J.J. Johnson

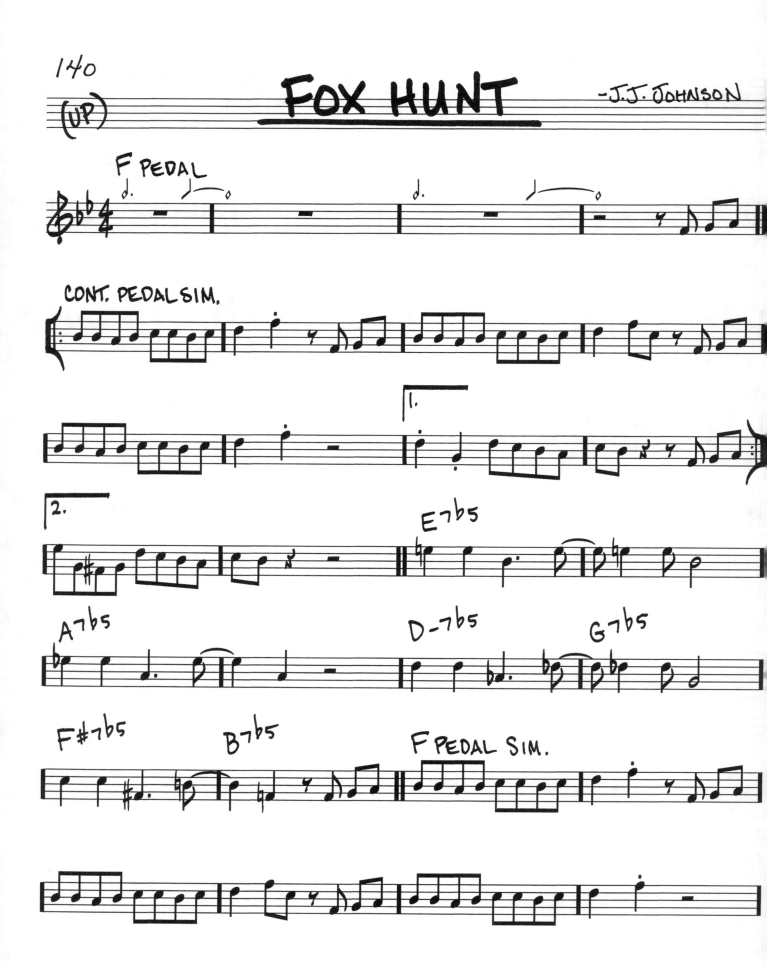

FINE

(TO SOLOS)

SOLOS RHYTHM CHANGES

Bb B°7 C-7 F7 | Bb B°7 C-7 F7 | Bb Bb7 Eb E°7 | Bb F7 Bb

E7b5 | A7b5 | D-7b5 G7b5 | F#7b5 B7b5

Bb B°7 C-7 F7 | Bb B°7 C-7 F7 | Bb Bb7 Eb E°7 | Bb F7 Bb

AFTER SOLOS, D.C. AL FINE

FRENESÍ

—Alberto Domínguez

(BOSSA)

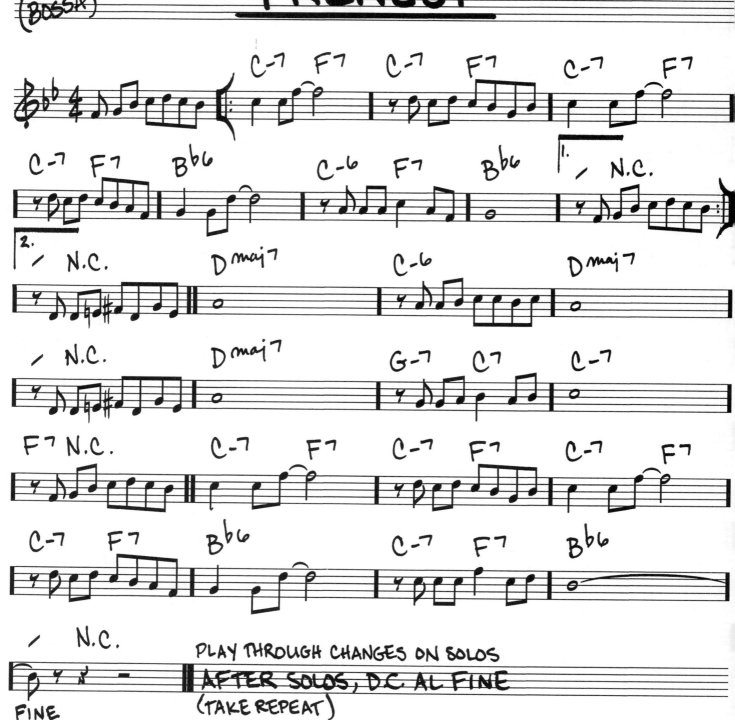

PLAY THROUGH CHANGES ON SOLOS
AFTER SOLOS, D.C. AL FINE
(TAKE REPEAT)

FINE

THE FRIM FRAM SAUCE

(EASY SWING)

—Joe Ricardel/Redd Evans

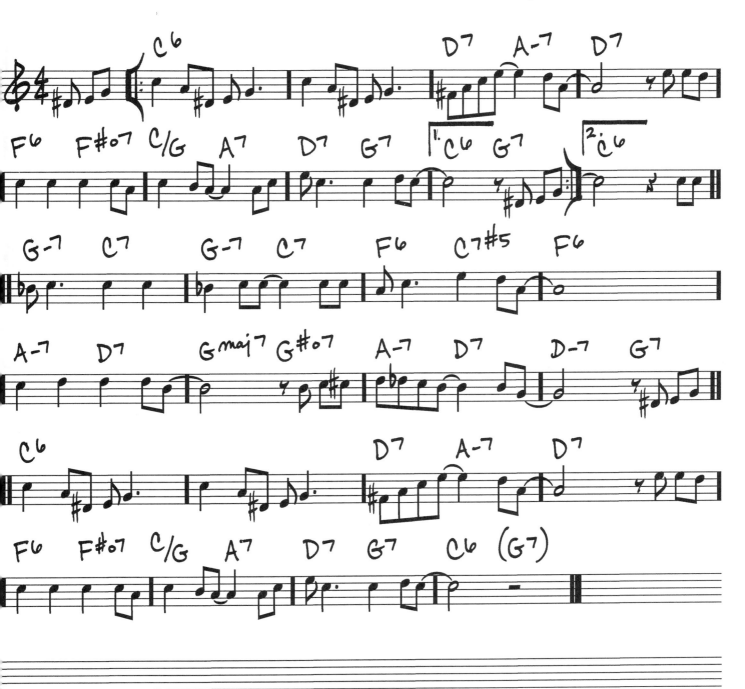

144

Funky

(MED. BLUES)

—Kenny Burrell

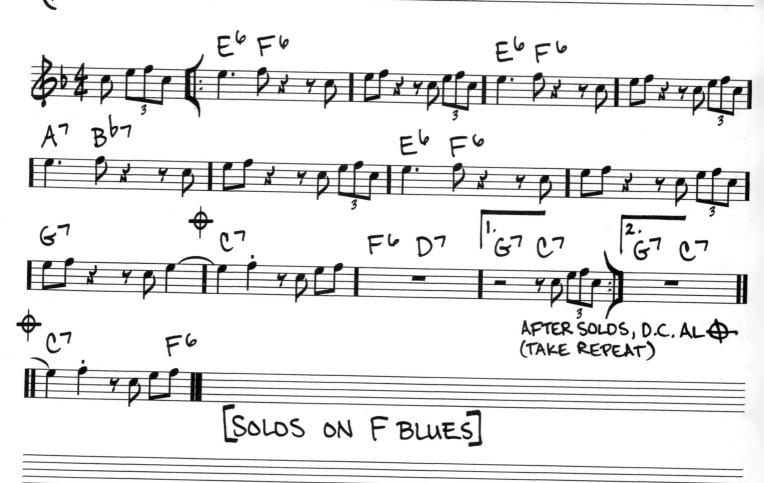

[SOLOS ON F BLUES]

AFTER SOLOS, D.C. AL ⊕
(TAKE REPEAT)

GEORGIA ON MY MIND

(BALLAD)

-Hoagy Carmichael/ Stuart Gorrell

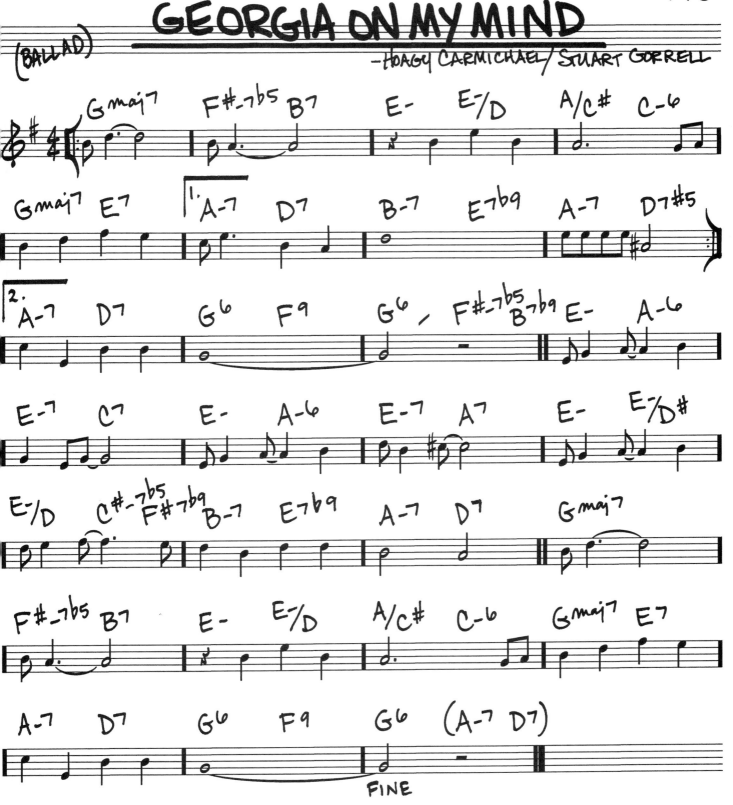

FINE

146

Get Me To The Church On Time

(BRIGHT)

-Alan Jay Lerner / Frederick Loewe

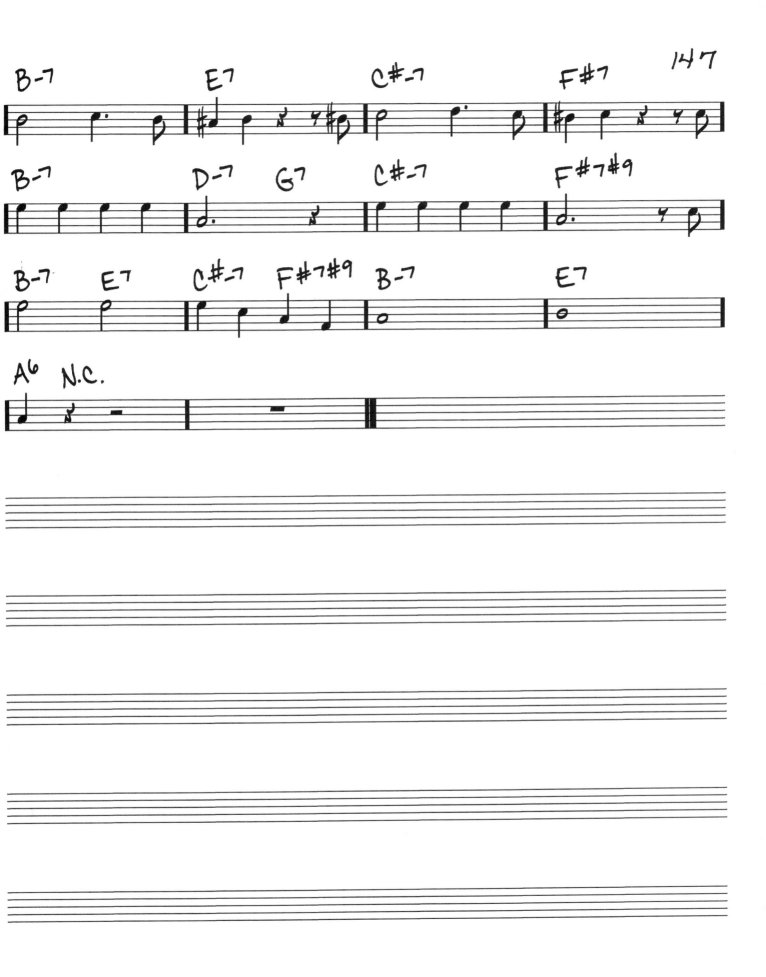

148

GET OUT OF TOWN
— COLE PORTER

(BALLAD)

GETTIN' IT TOGETHA
—Bobby Timmons

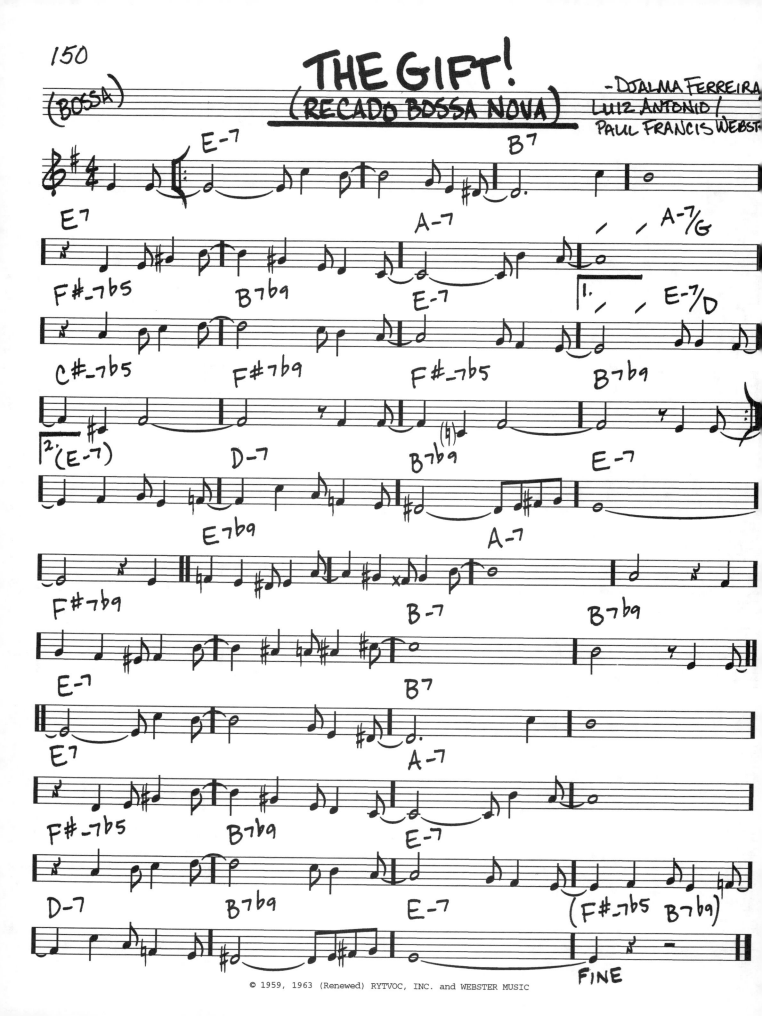

GIRL TALK

— Neal Hefti

[SOLOS — TAKE 1st ENDING ONLY]

152

GRAVY WALTZ

— Ray Brown/ Steve Allen

(Med.)

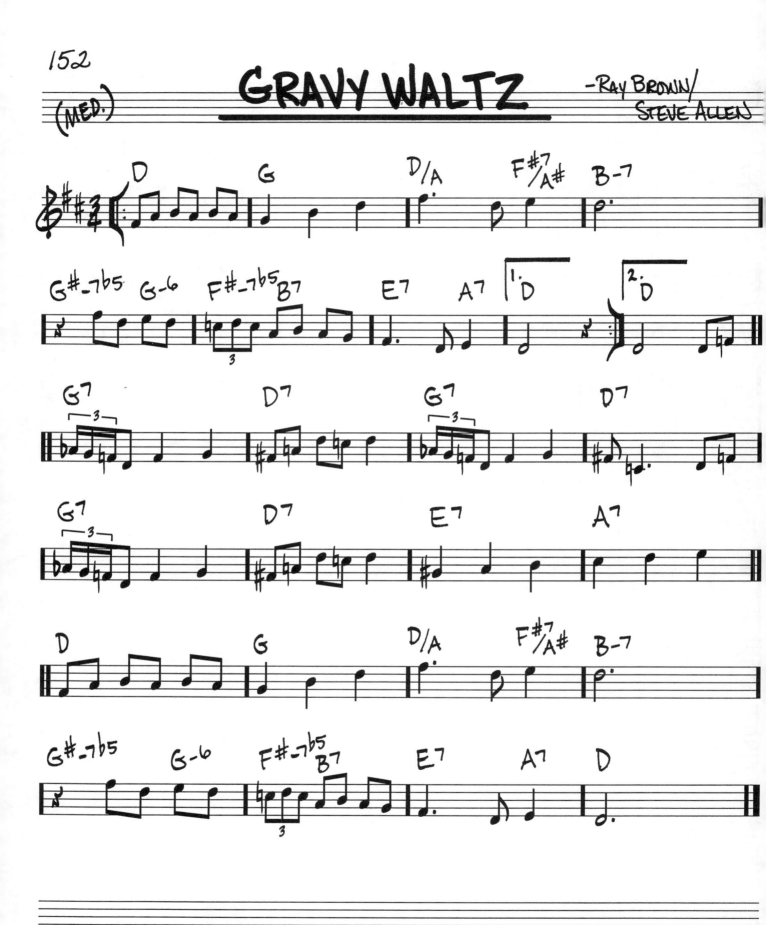

154

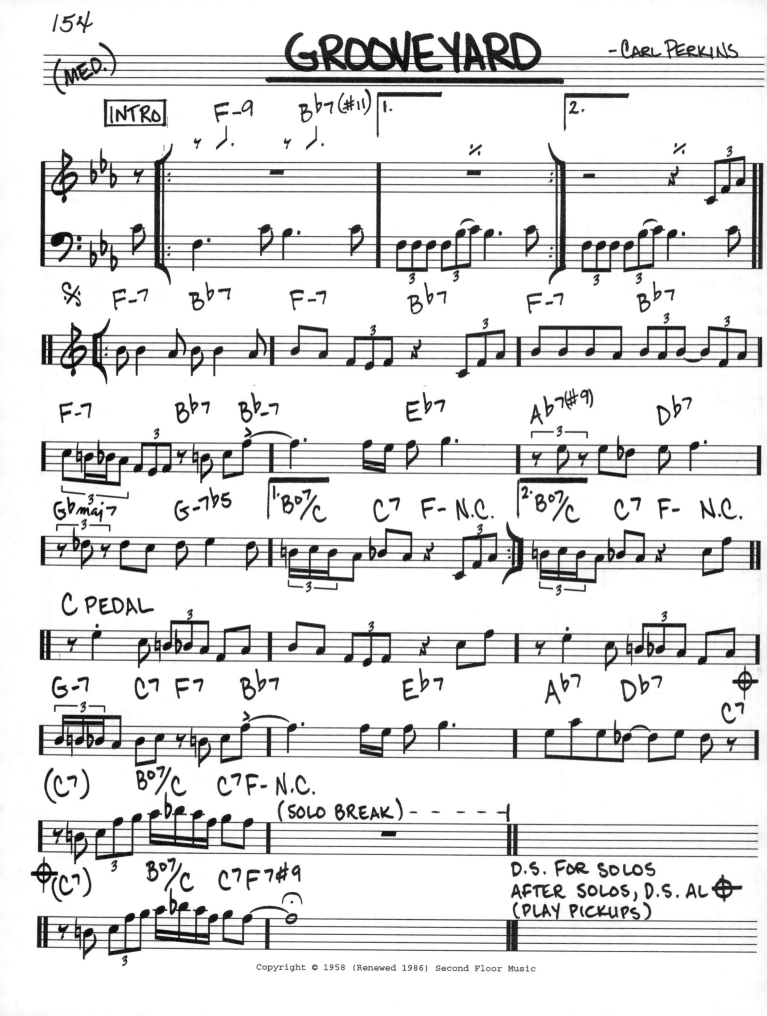

HACKENSACK

-THELONIOUS MONK

(MED. UP SWING)

HALLUCINATIONS

—Earl "Bud" Powell

(Fast Bop)

SOLO A B C
AFTER SOLOS, D.C. AL FINE

HAPPY LITTLE SUNBEAM

-Russell Freeman

HAVONA

158
(BRIGHT SAMBA)
EVEN 8ths

—Jaco Pastorius

HEAD AND SHOULDERS

— CEDAR WALTON

HIGH FLY
— Randy Weston

(MED. SWING)

162

HI BECK

—LEE KONITZ

(MED. UP)

SOLOS

| Dmaj7 | F#-7 F°7 | E-7 | A7 | Dmaj7 | F#-7 F°7 | E-7 | A7 |
| //// | //// | //// | //// | //// | //// | //// | //// |

| D7 | | Gmaj7 | | E7 | | E-7 | A7 |
| //// | //// | //// | //// | //// | //// | //// | //// |

| Dmaj7 | F#-7 F°7 | E-7 | A7 | A-7 | D7 | Gmaj7 | |
| //// | //// | //// | //// | //// | //// | //// | //// |

| Gmaj7 | C7 | F#-7 | B7 | E-7 | A7 | Dmaj7 | E-7 A7 |
| //// | //// | //// | //// | //// | //// | //// | //// |

HOCUS-POCUS

— LEE MORGAN

(MED. UP SWING)

(LAST x)
NO ANTICIPATIONS ON SOLOS

HOLY LAND

— CEDAR WALTON

(MED.)

HONEYSUCKLE ROSE

(MED.)

— Thomas "Fats" Waller/ Andy Razaf

HORACE SCOPE

-Horace Silver

(MED.)

TAKE 1ST ENDING ON SOLOS
DURING SOLOS: BASS WALKS, NO CHORD ANTICIPATION
AFTER SOLOS, D.C. AL ⊕, TAKE REPEAT

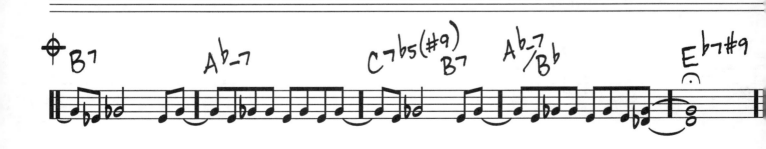

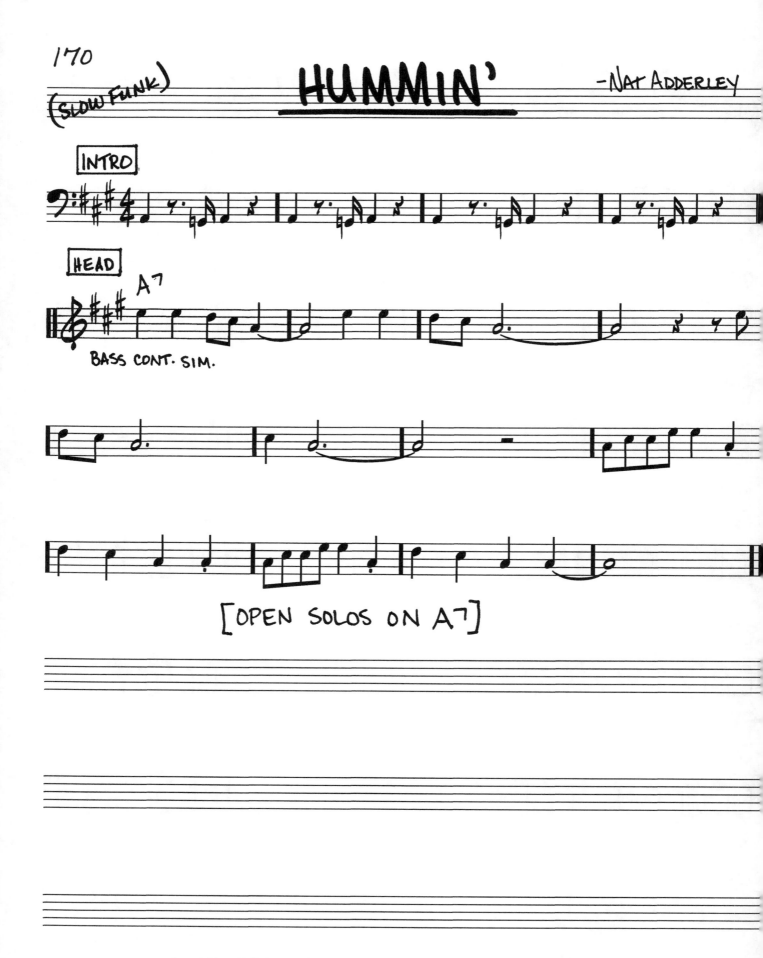

[OPEN SOLOS ON A7]

HUMPTY DUMPTY

—Chick Corea

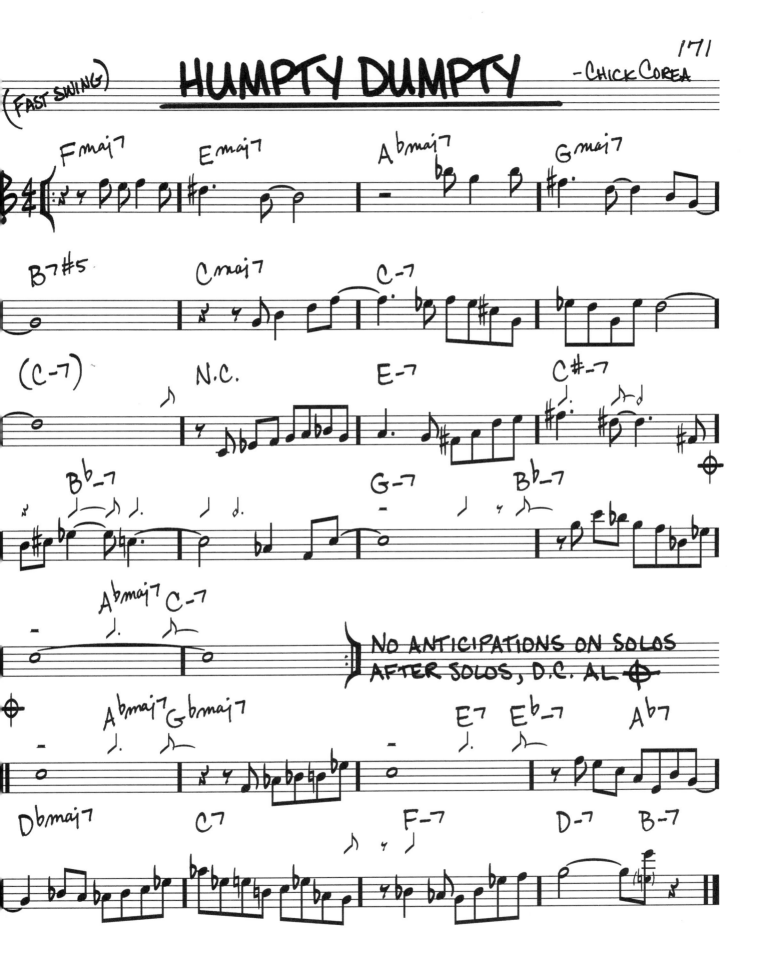

NO ANTICIPATIONS ON SOLOS
AFTER SOLOS, D.C. AL ⊕

172

I BELIEVE IN YOU — Frank Loesser

(MED. UP)

I DON'T STAND A GHOST OF A CHANCE

-Victor Young/Bing Crosby/Ned Washington

(MED. OR BALLAD)

I GET ALONG WITHOUT YOU VERY WELL
(EXCEPT SOMETIMES)

-HOAGY CARMICHAEL

I HEAR A RHAPSODY

George Frajos/
Jack Baker/
Dick Gasparre

(Med. Swing)

I REMEMBER YOU

Victor Schertzinger/ Johnny Mercer

(MED.)

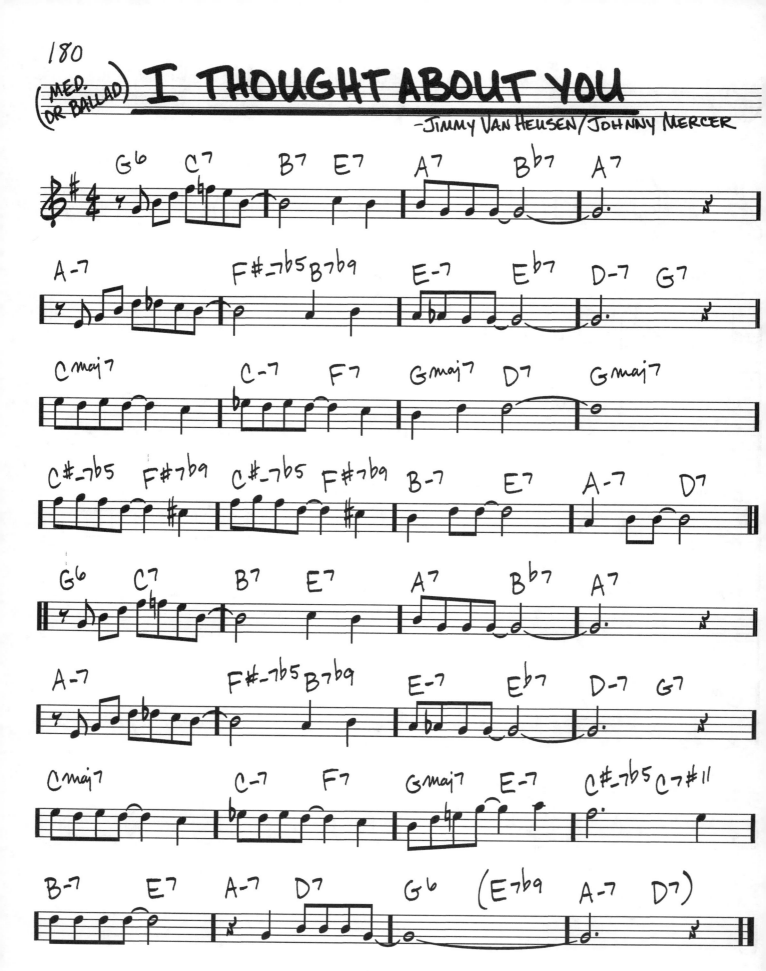

I Will Wait For You

(MED. OR BALLAD)

—Michel Legrand / Jacques Demy / Norman Gimbel

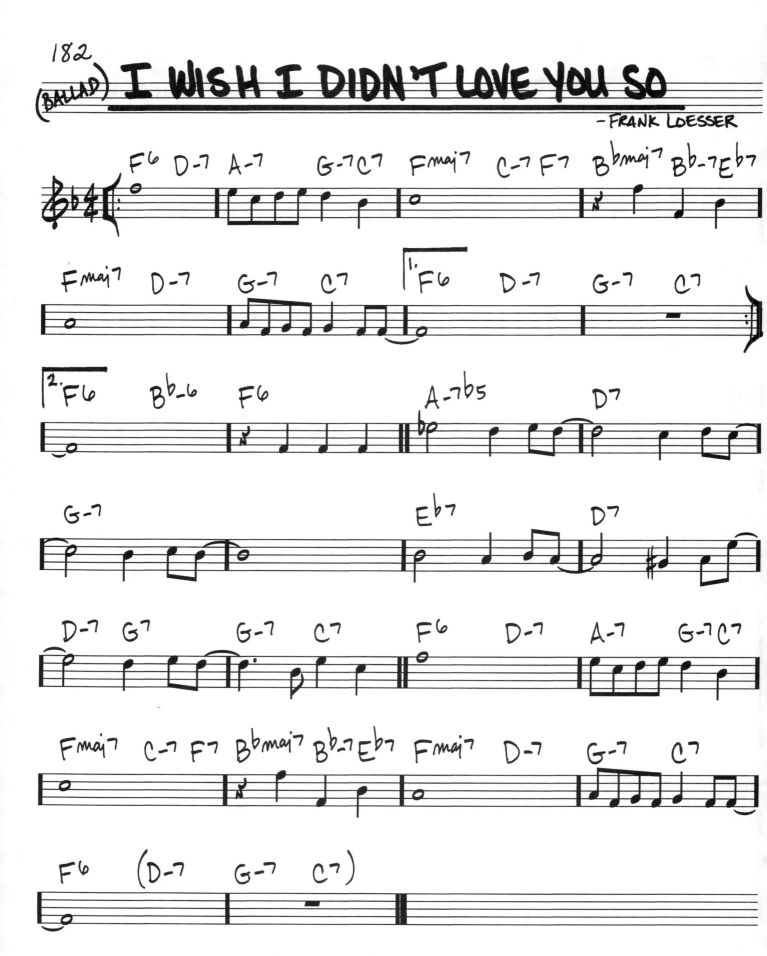

I'LL KNOW

—Frank Loesser

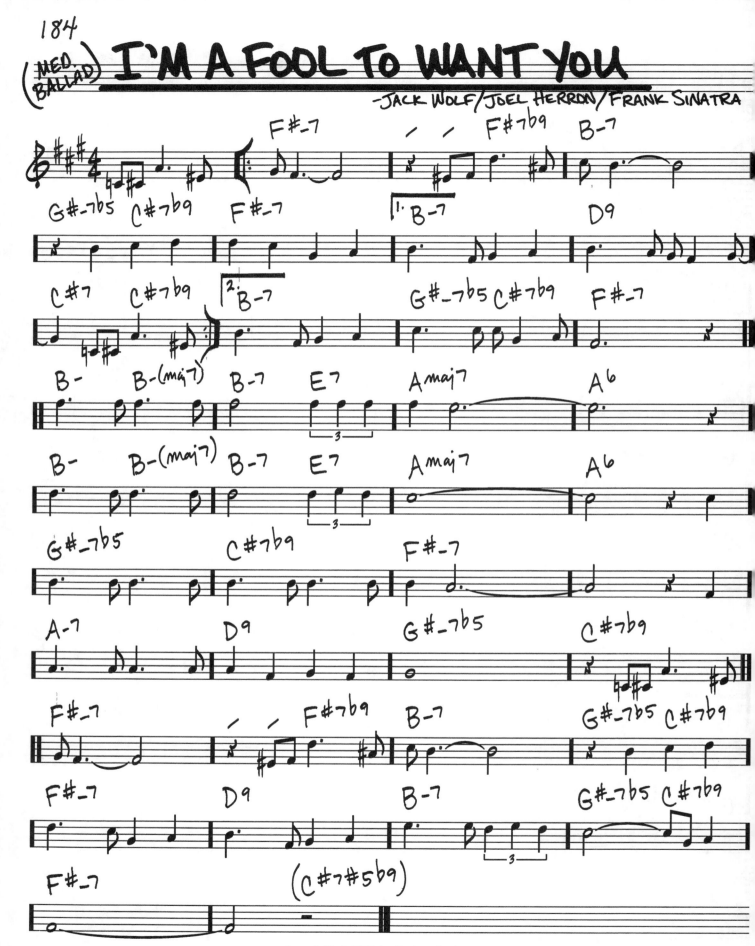

I'M CONFESSIN' (THAT I LOVE YOU)

(MED. BALLAD)

-Al Neiburg/Doc Dougherty/Ellis Reynolds

186

(MED.) **I'M JUST A LUCKY SO AND SO**

-Duke Ellington / Mack David

(ED) I'M PUTTING ALL MY EGGS IN ONE BASKET

-IRVING BERLIN

I'VE FOUND A NEW BABY
(I FOUND A NEW BABY)

188

(MED.)

-Jack Palmer/ Spencer Williams

I'VE TOLD EV'RY LITTLE STAR

-Jerome Kern/Oscar Hammerstein II

190

Idol Gossip

-Gerry Mulligan

192
(BALLAD)
(OR MED.)

If I Loved You

—Richard Rodgers/
Oscar Hammerstein II

IF I SHOULD LOSE YOU

(MED.)

— LEO ROBIN / RALPH RAINGER

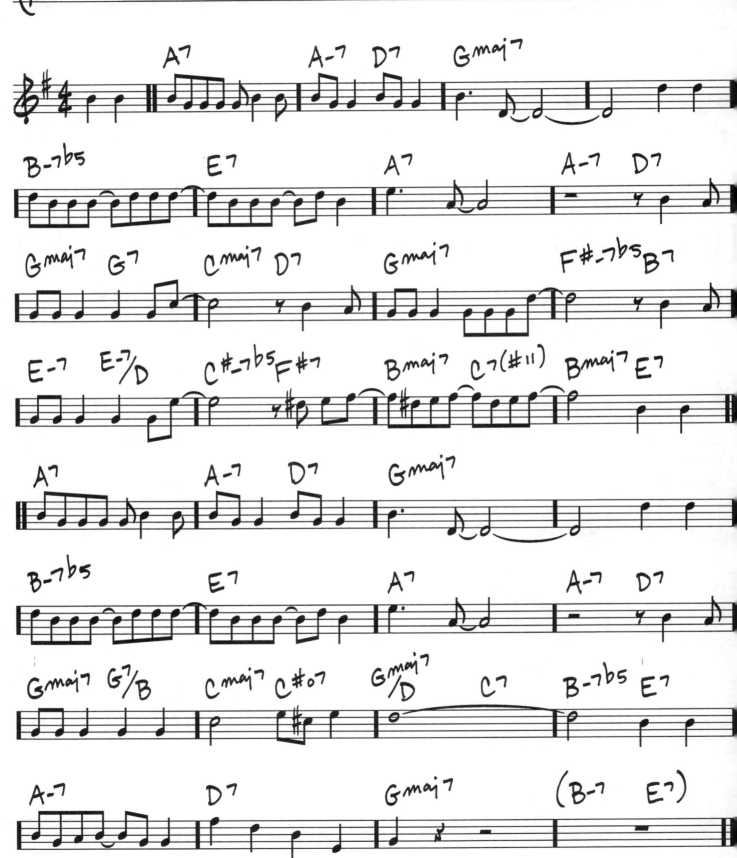

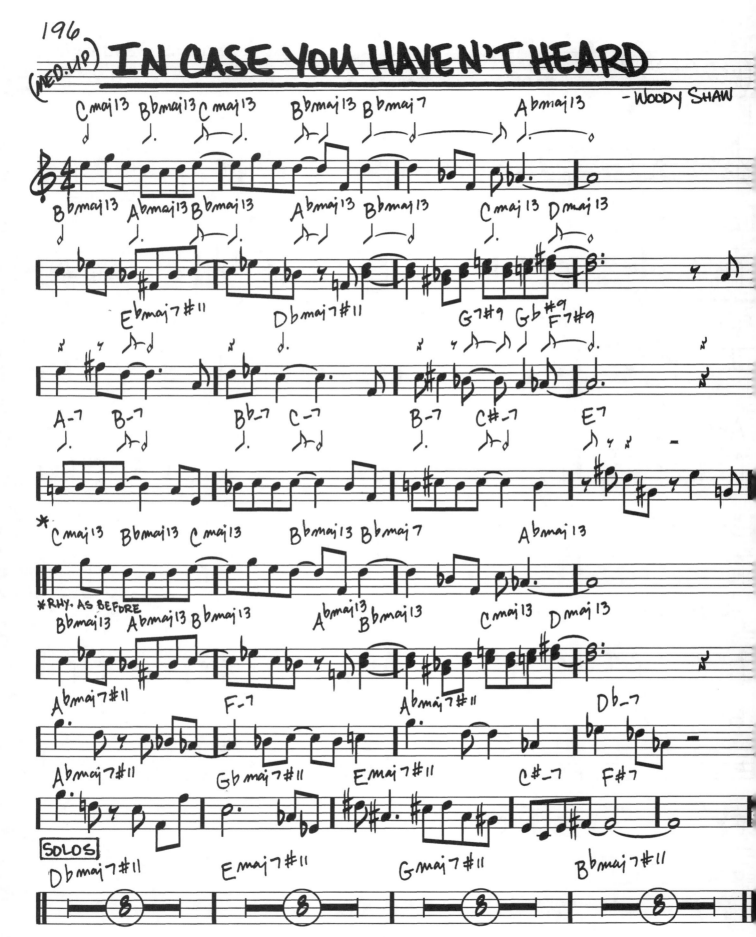

196

IN CASE YOU HAVEN'T HEARD

(MED.UP)

— WOODY SHAW

In the Still of the Night

(BRIGHT SWING)

- Cole Porter

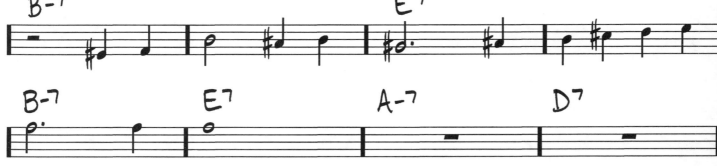

INDIANA
(BACK HOME AGAIN IN INDIANA)

-JAMES F. HANLEY/BALLARD MACDONALD

(UPSWING)

ISLAND BIRDIE

—McCoy Tyner

(CALYPSO)

(MED.)

IT COULD HAPPEN TO YOU

-JAMES VAN HEUS
JOHNNY BURK

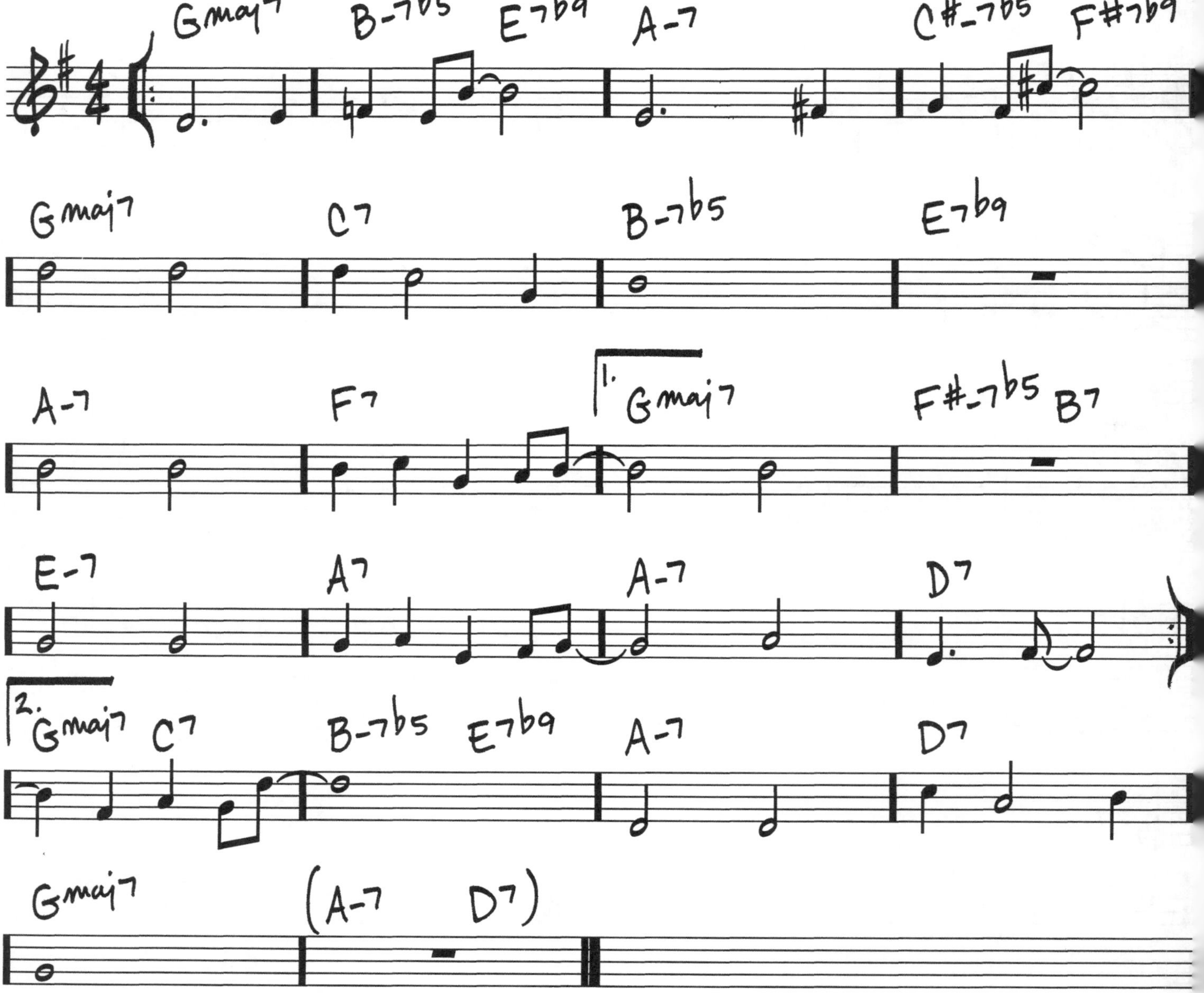

It Might As Well Be Spring

(Ballad)

-Richard Rodgers/Oscar Hammerstein II

It Will Have To Do Until The Real Thing Comes Along

(Ballad)

-Mann Holiner/Alberta Nichols/Saul Chaplin/L.E. Freeman/Sammy Cahn

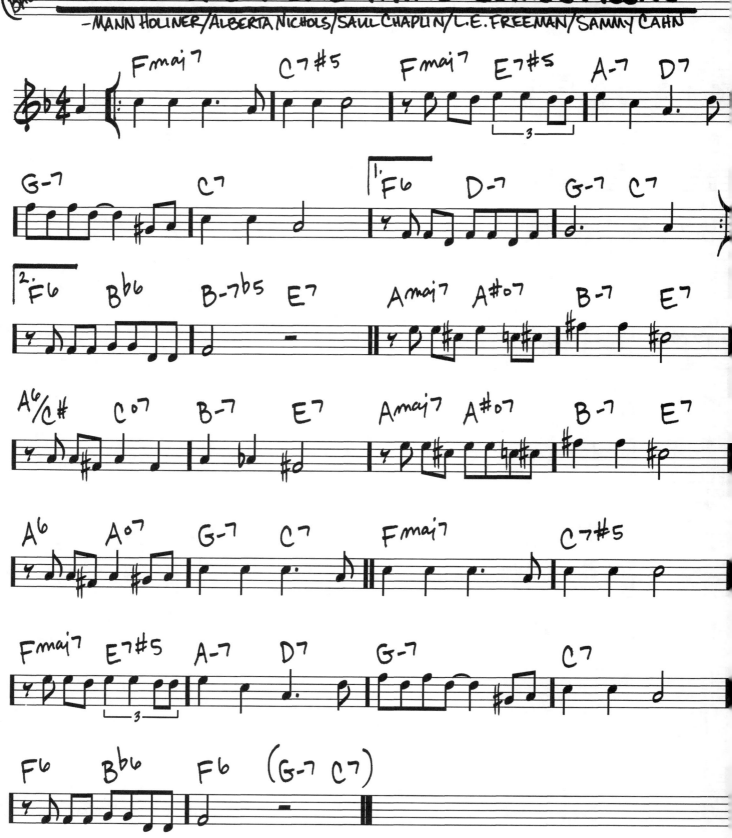

IT'S A BLUE WORLD

-Bob Wright/
Chet Forrest

208
(MED. UP SWING) **It's All Right With Me** —Cole Porter

SOLO ON ENTIRE FORM

IT'S ONLY A PAPER MOON

(MED.)

—Harold Arlen/
Billy Rose/
E.Y. Harburg

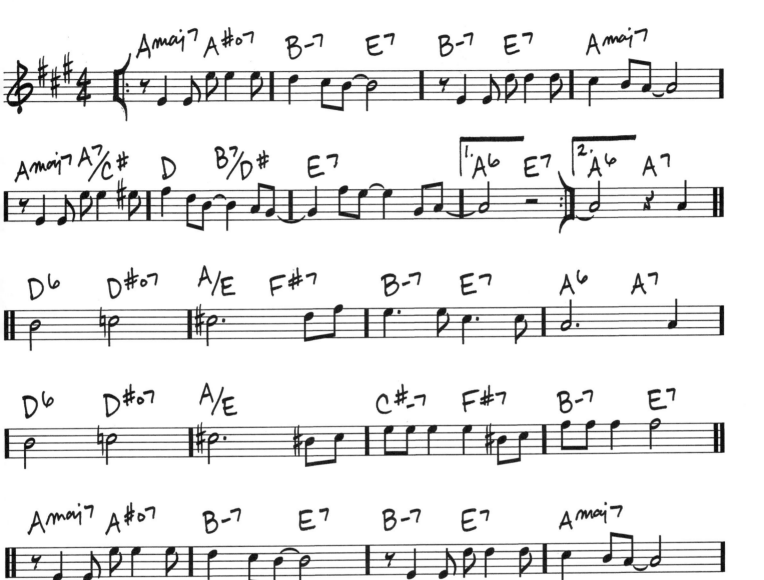

210

(SLOW SWING) **It's So Peaceful In The Country**

-Alec Wilder

JACKIE

— Hampton Hawes

(BRIGHT BLUES)

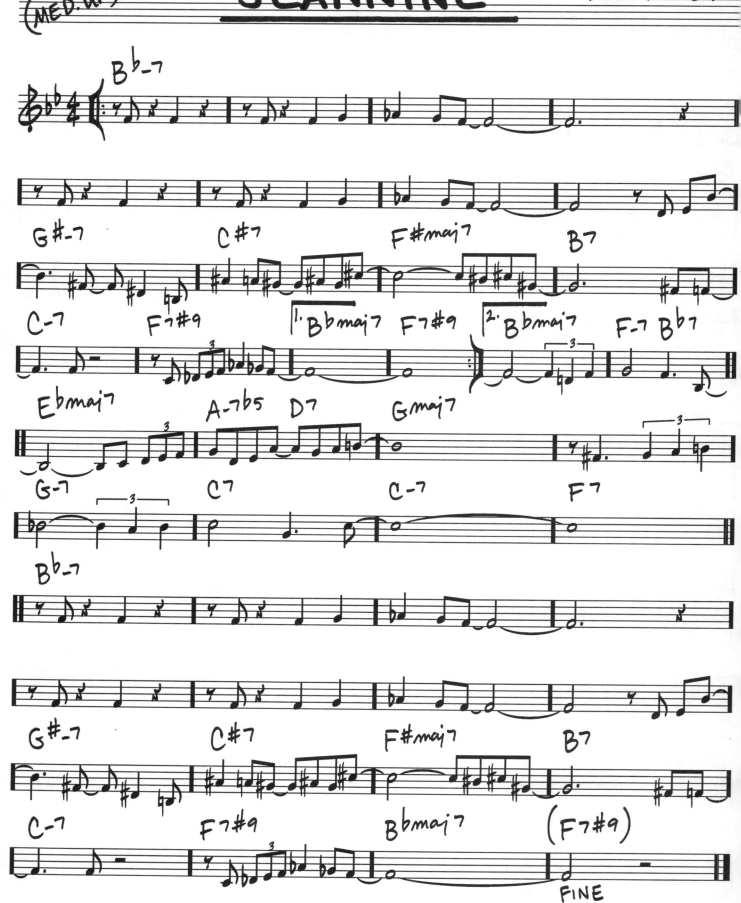

Jingles

—John L. (Wes) Montgomery

(MED.)

JITTERBUG WALTZ

—THOMAS "FATS" WALLER

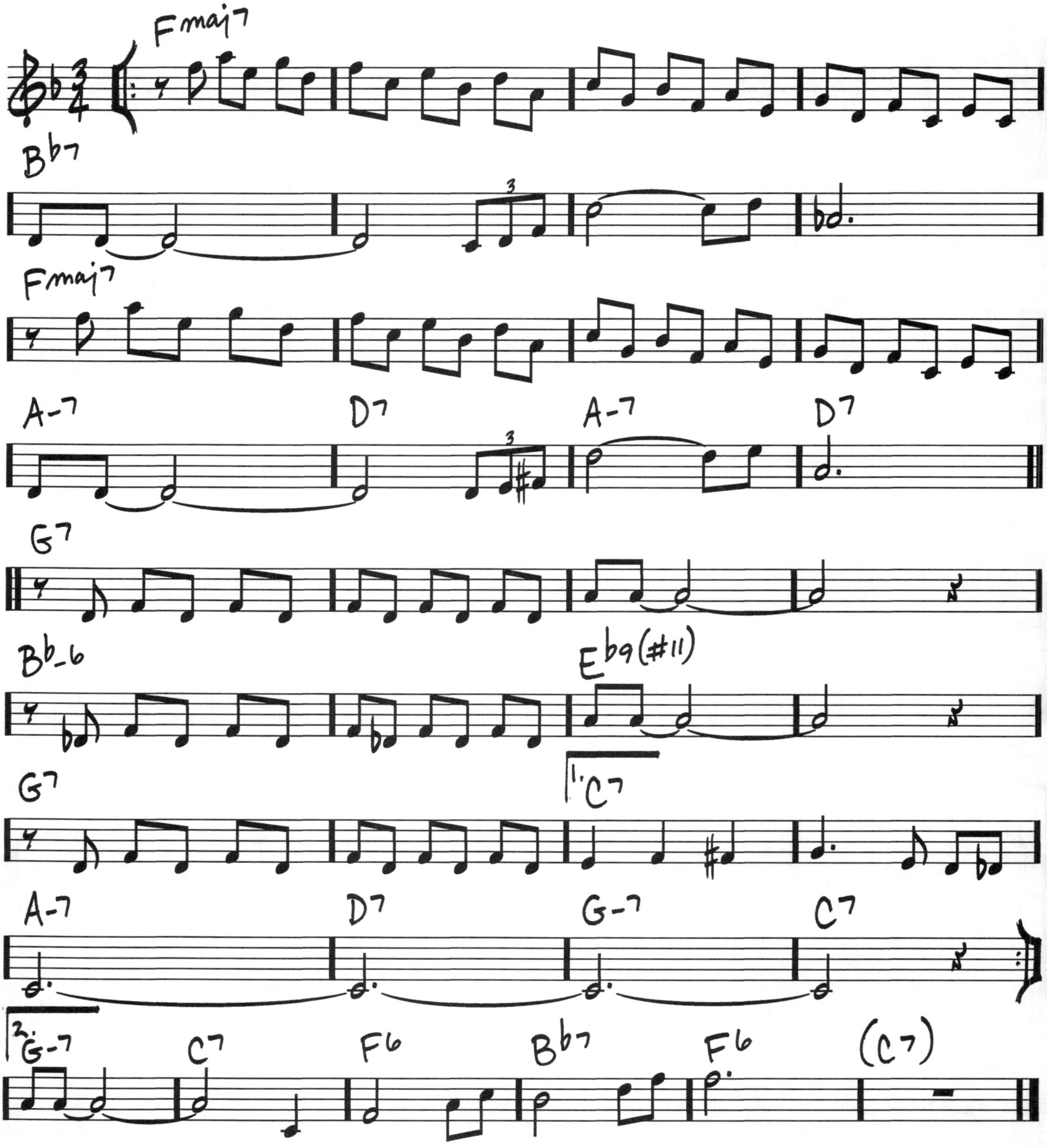

215

(FUNKY BLUES)

THE JODY GRIND
—Horace Silver

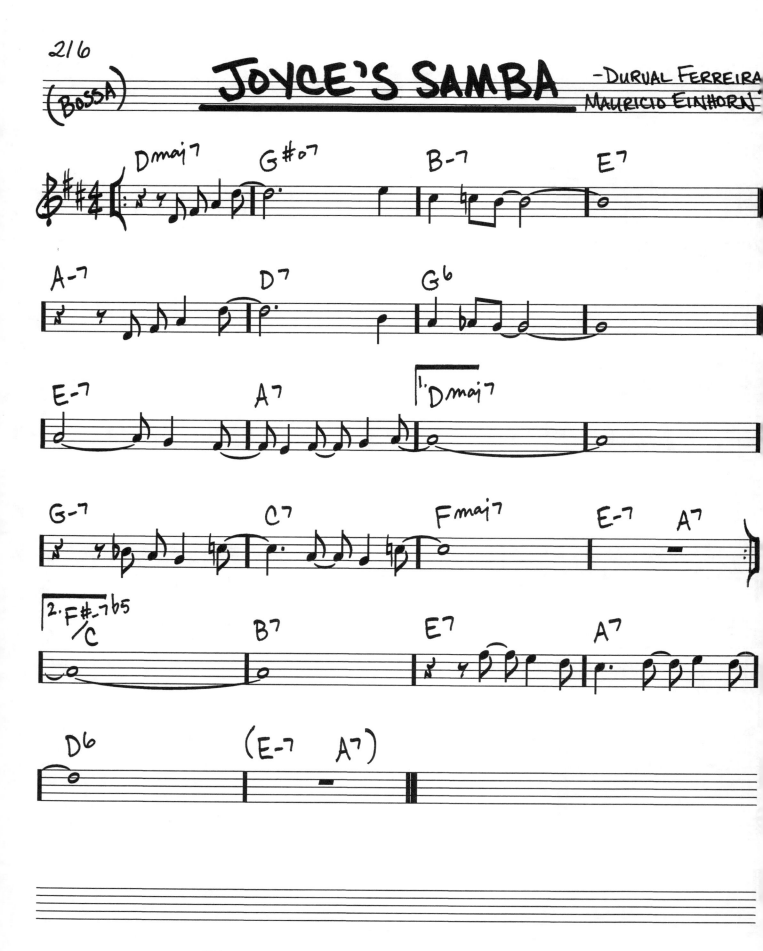

Joyce's Samba

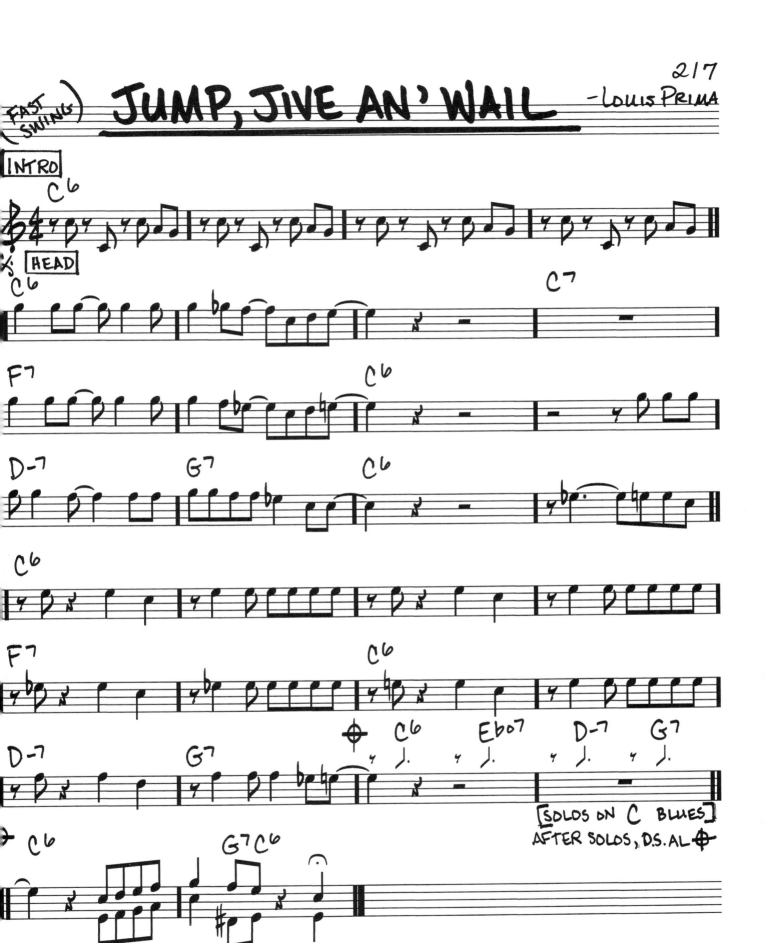

(MED.) JUST A SETTIN' AND A ROCKIN'

-Duke Ellington / Billy Strayhorn

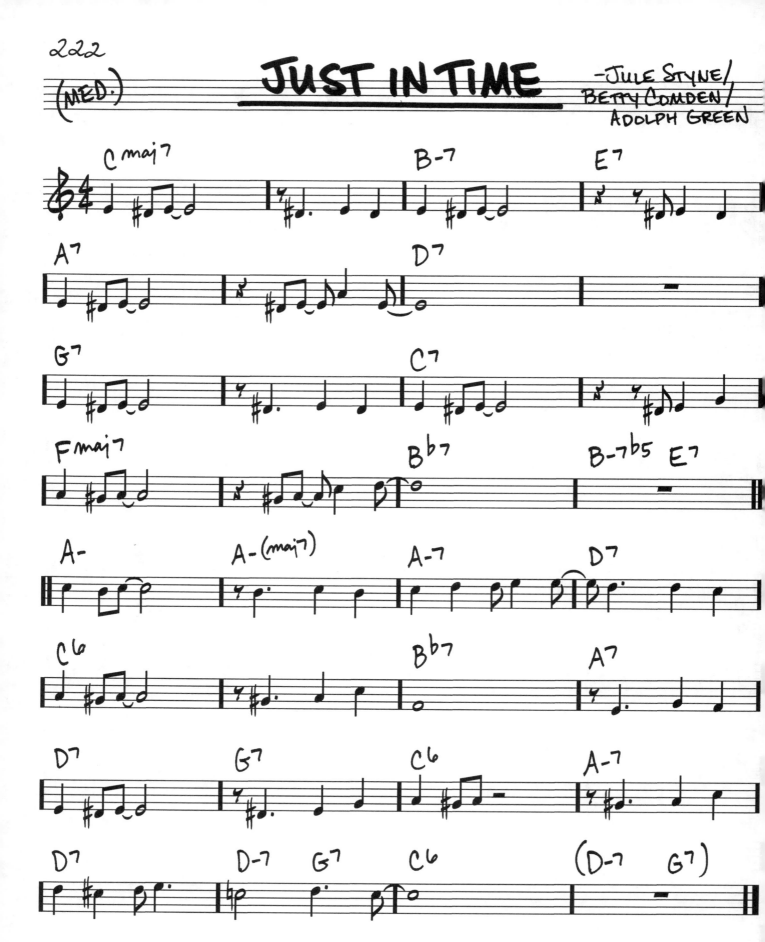

Just in Time

KARY'S TRANCE

223

-Lee Konitz

(MED. UP)

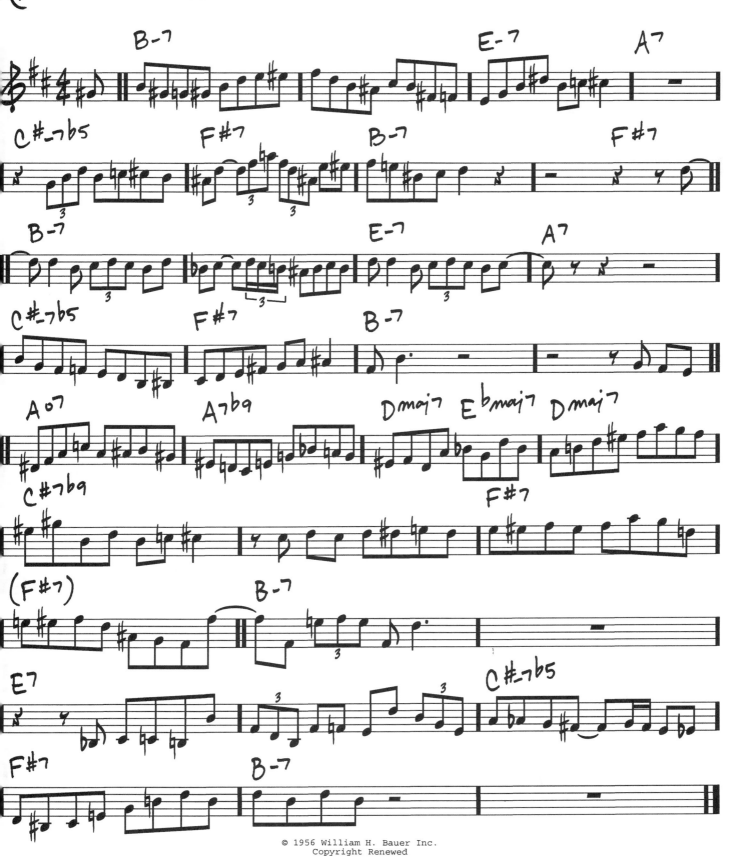

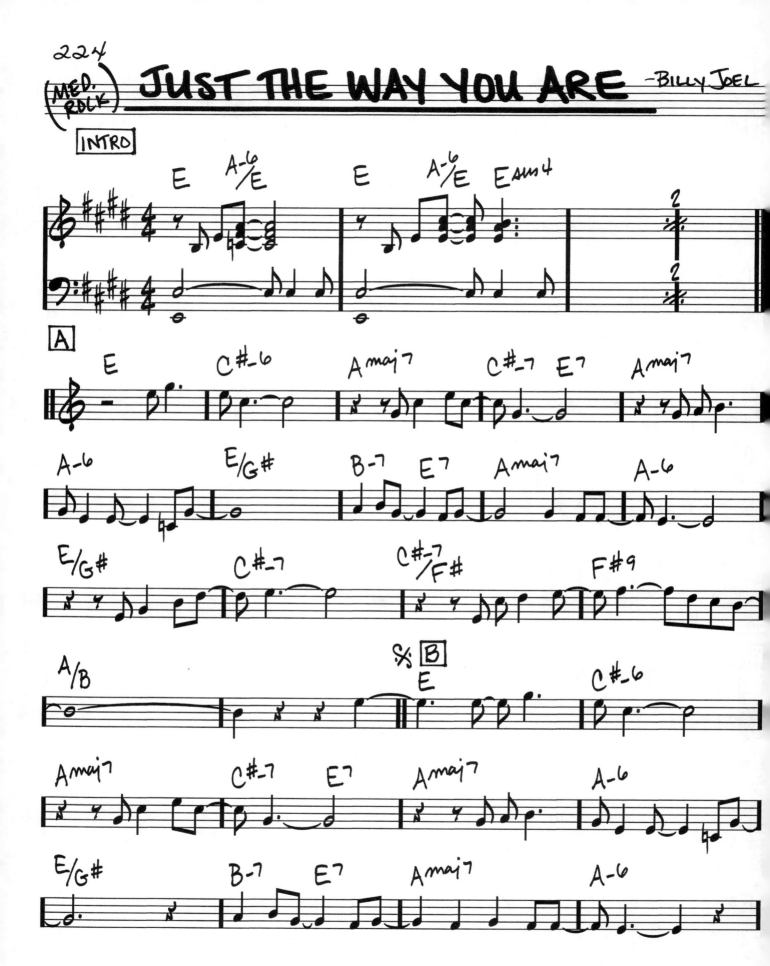

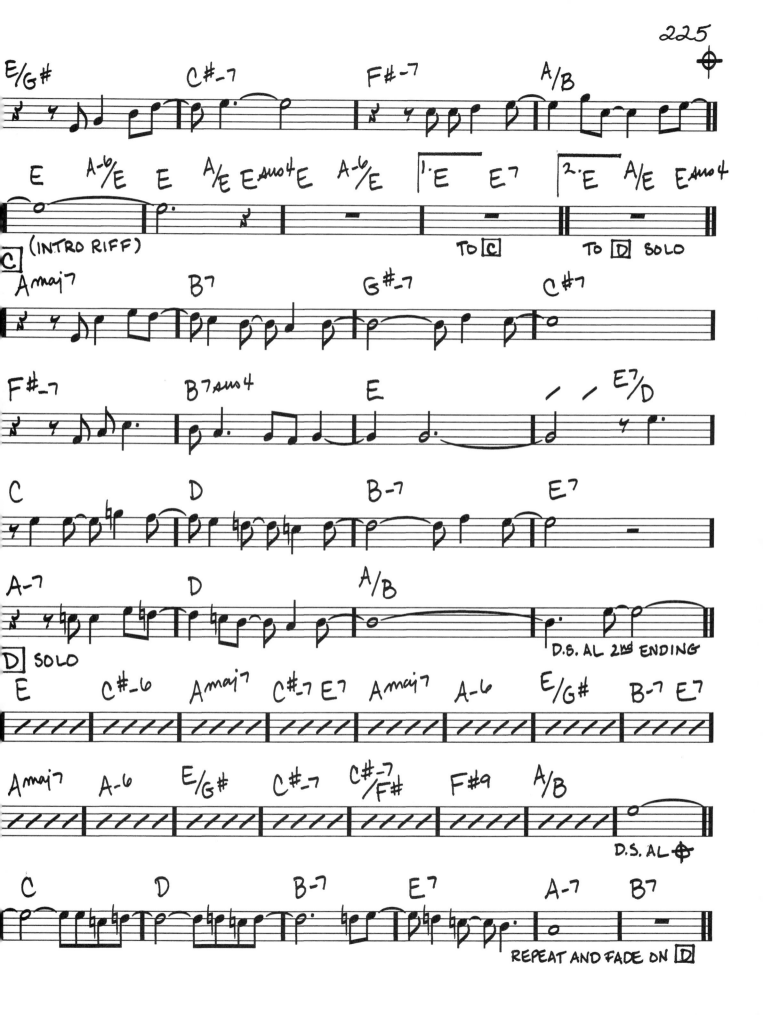

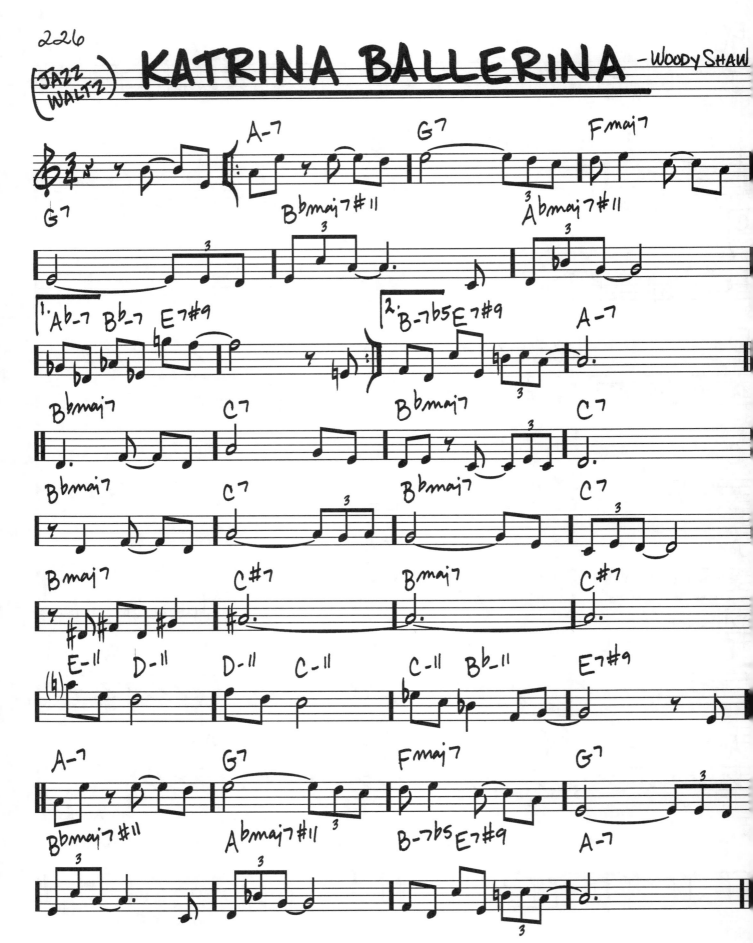

226

THE KICKER

-Joe Henderson

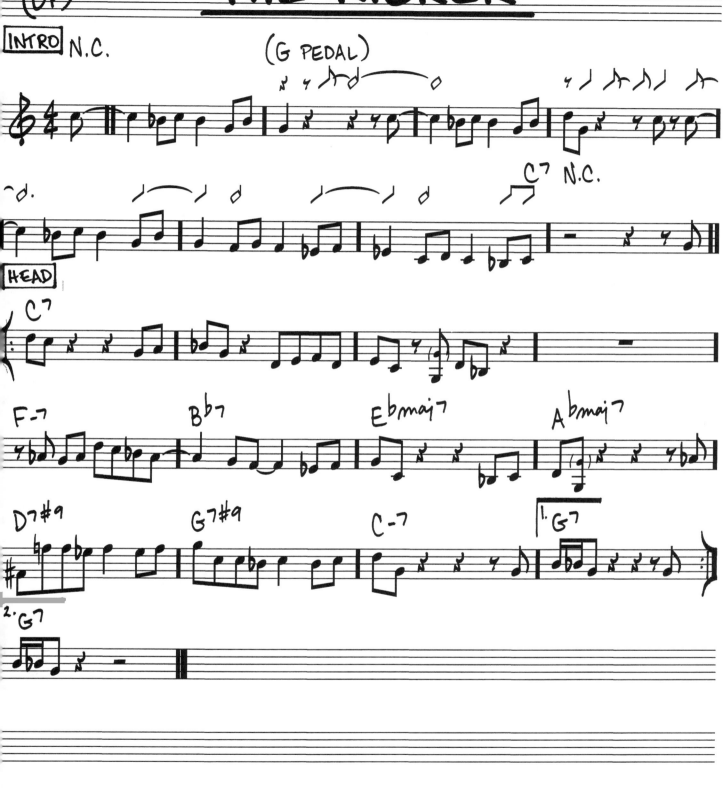

KIDS ARE PRETTY PEOPLE
(MED. SLOW)
—THAD JONES

228

Killer Joe

—Benny Golson

(MED.)

AFTER SOLOS, LAST HEAD,
VAMP INTRO TILL FADE

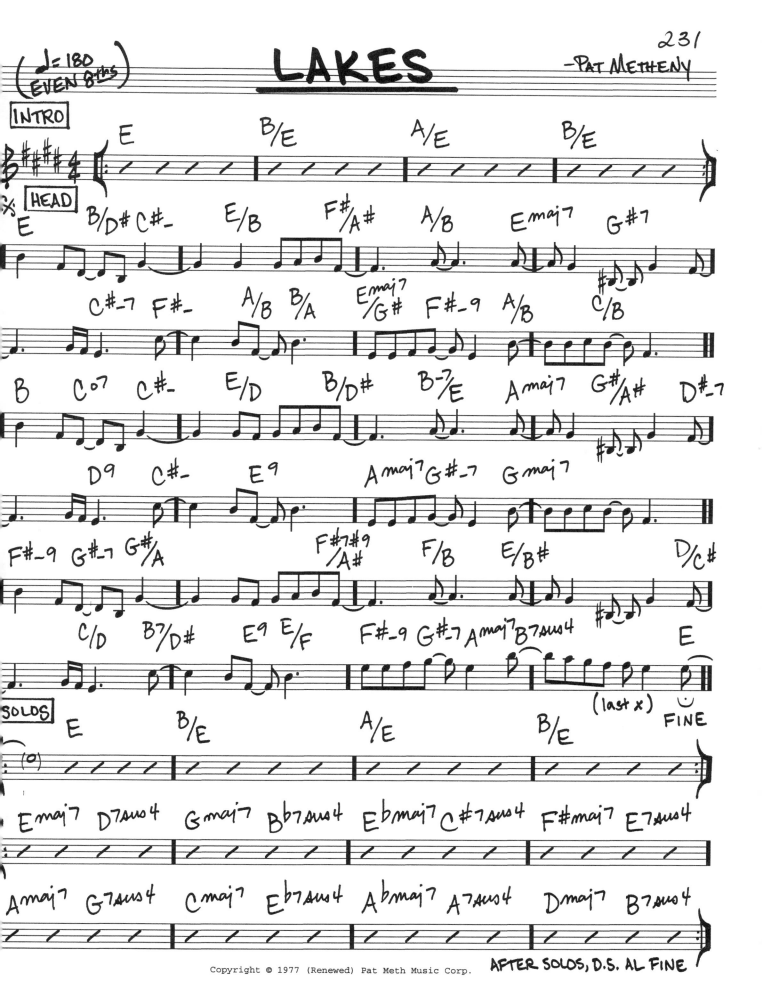

LAKES

—Pat Metheny

AFTER SOLOS, D.S. AL FINE

THE LAST TIME I SAW PARIS

-Jerome Kern/Oscar Hammerstein II

(MED.)

234

LEILA

(SLOW SWING)

—John L. (Wes) Montgomery

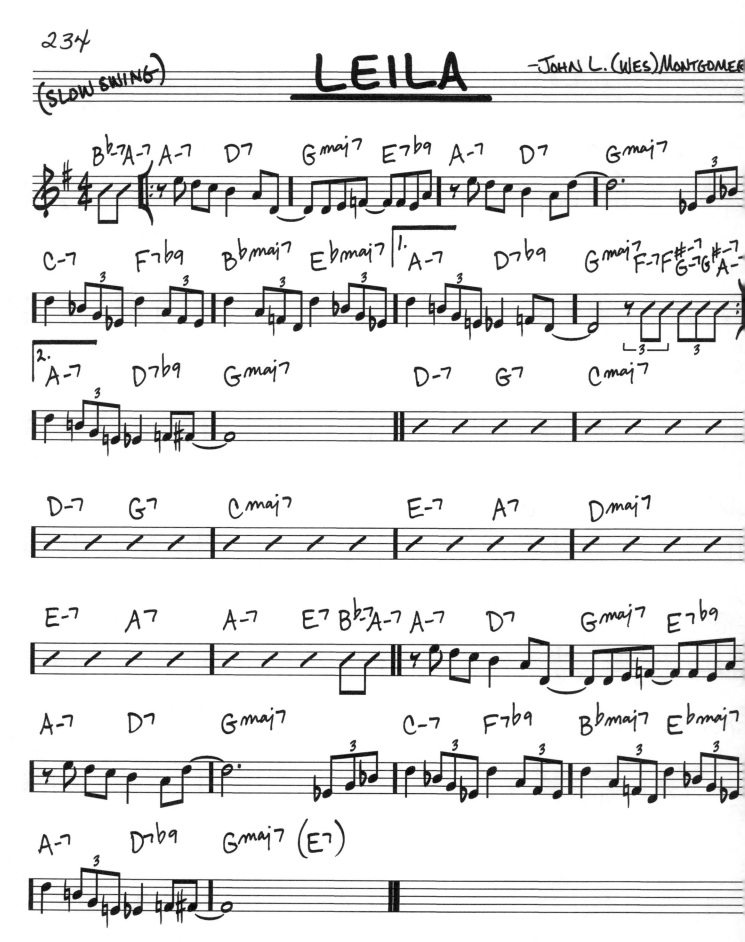

LENNIE'S PENNIES

-Lennie Tristano

(FAST SWING)

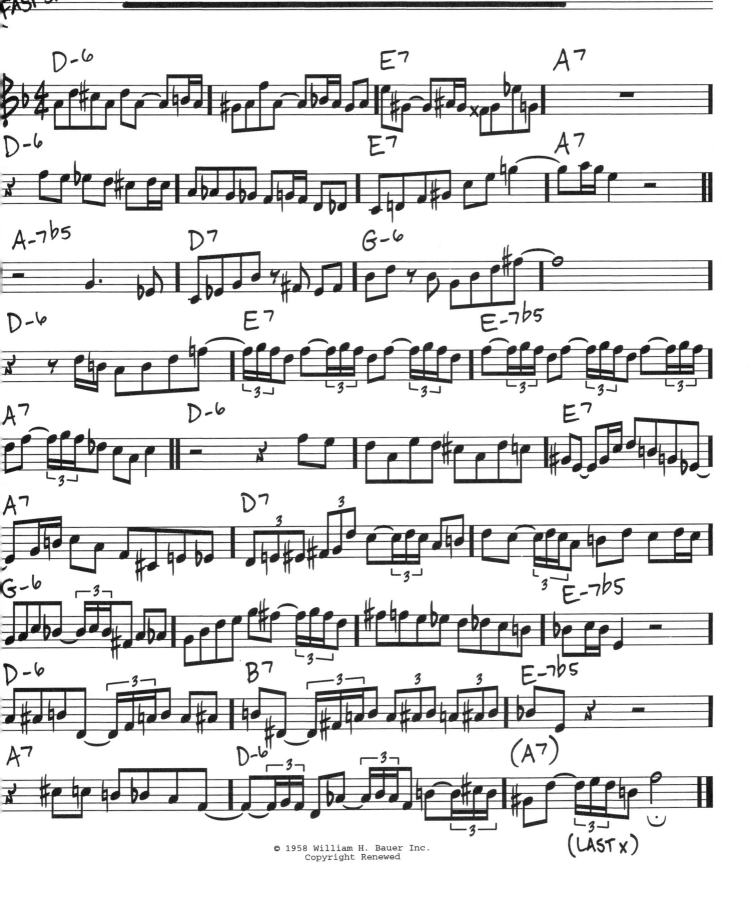

LET'S COOL ONE

— Thelonious Monk

(MED. SWING)

LET'S FALL IN LOVE

— HAROLD ARLEN/
TED KOEHLER

(MED.)

LET'S GET LOST

(MED.)

— Jimmy McHugh/ Frank Loesser

LIKE SONNY
(SIMPLE LIKE)

—John Coltrane

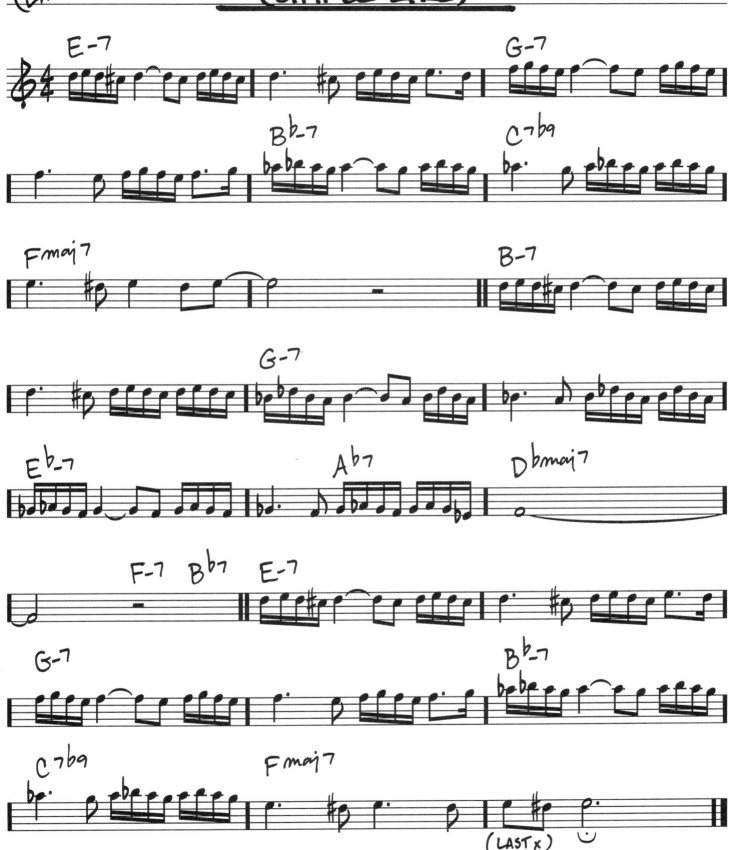

240

Little Chicago Fire — Frank Foster

242 (♩=216) (FAST)

LOCOMOTION

245 — John Coltrane

(FAST BLUES)

Copyright © 1957 (Renewed 1985) JOWCOL MUSIC

246

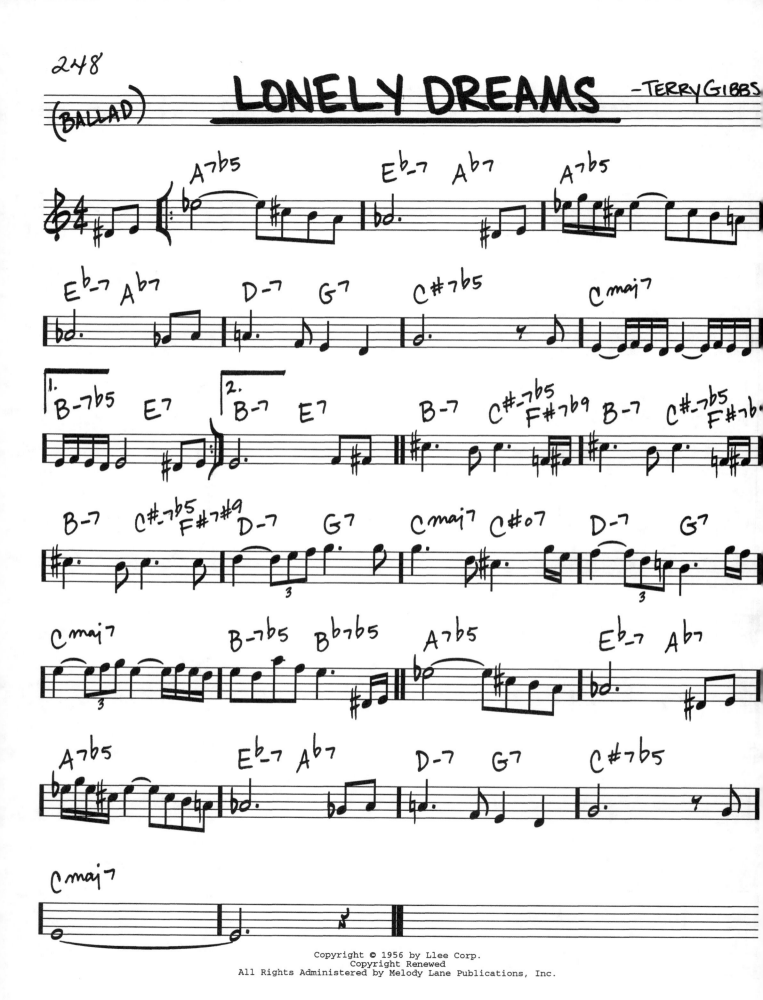

248

(BALLAD)

LONELY DREAMS

—Terry Gibbs

(MED.) LOOK FOR THE SILVER LINING

-JEROME KERN/BUDDY DESYLVA

(MED.) LOVE IS JUST AROUND THE CORNER

— LEO ROBIN / LEWIS E. GENSLER

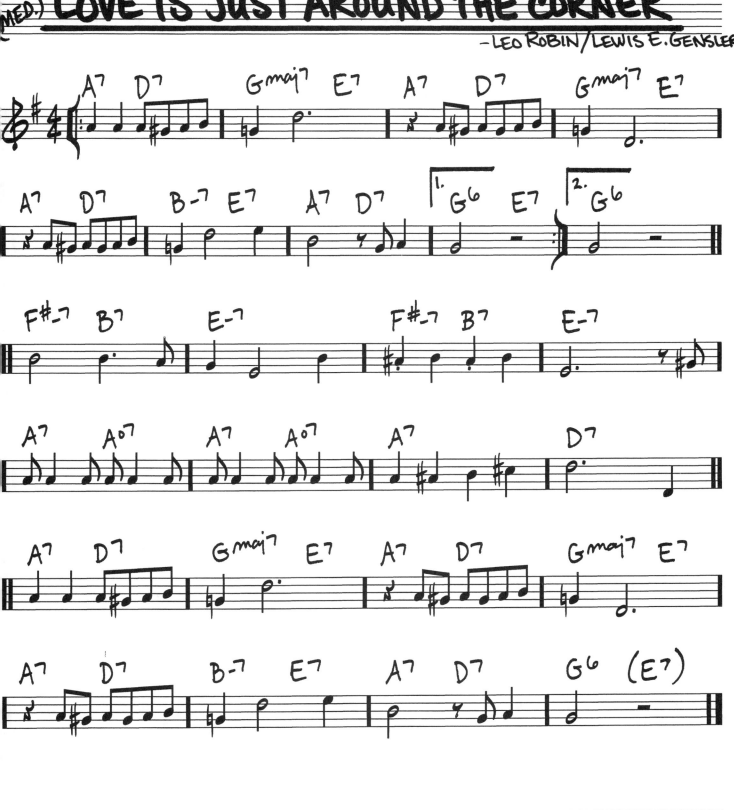

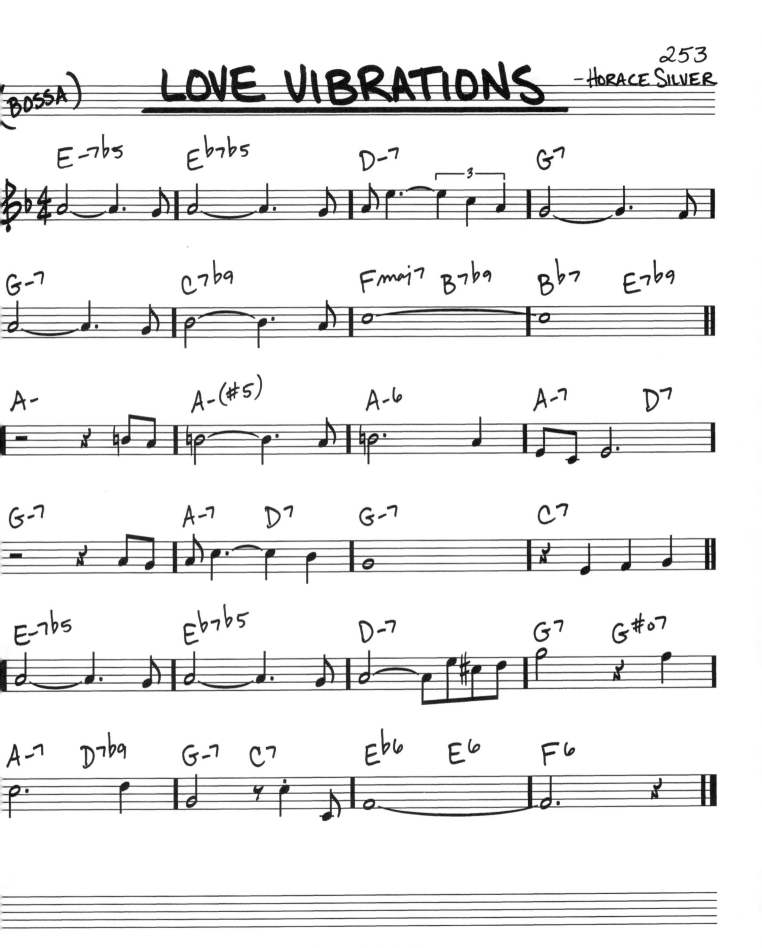

(BALLAD) A Lovely Way To Spend An Evening

-Jimmy McHugh/Harold Adamson

LOVER MAN
(OH, WHERE CAN YOU BE?)

(BALLAD)

— Jimmy Davis/
Roger Ramirez/
Jimmy Sherman

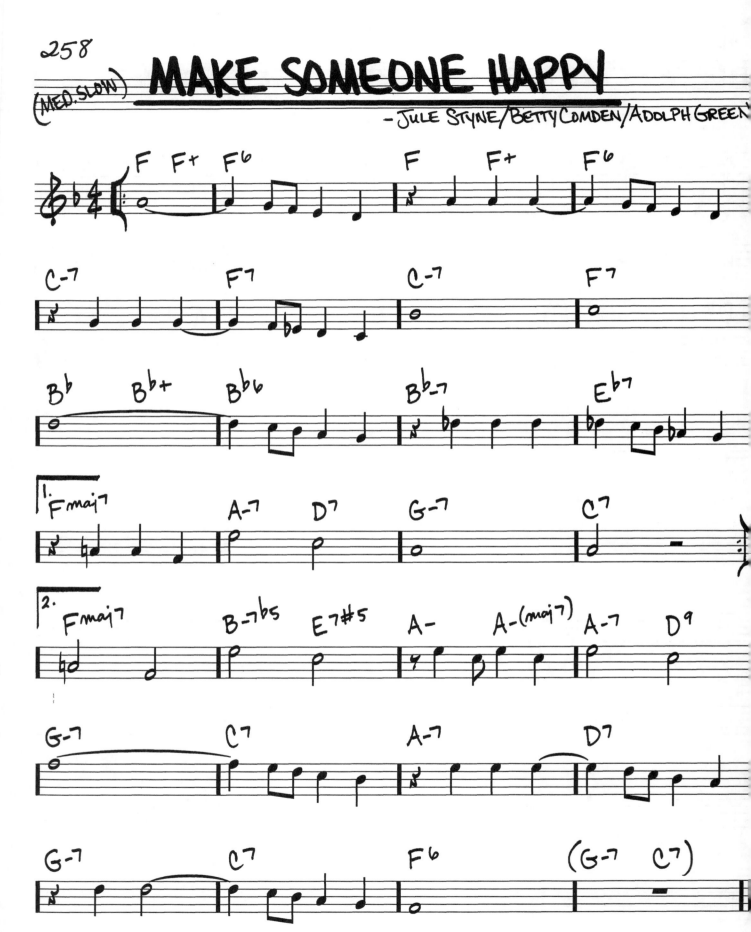

MAKE SOMEONE HAPPY

— Jule Styne / Betty Comden / Adolph Green

MANTECA

-Dizzy Gillespie/
Walter Gil Fuller/
Luciano Pozo Gonzales

(MED. LATIN)

MENINA FLOR

Luiz Bonfa / Maria Toledo

261

(Bossa)

264

MILES AHEAD

— Miles Davis

(MED. SWING)

MINOR MOOD

(MED.)

-CLIFFORD BROWN

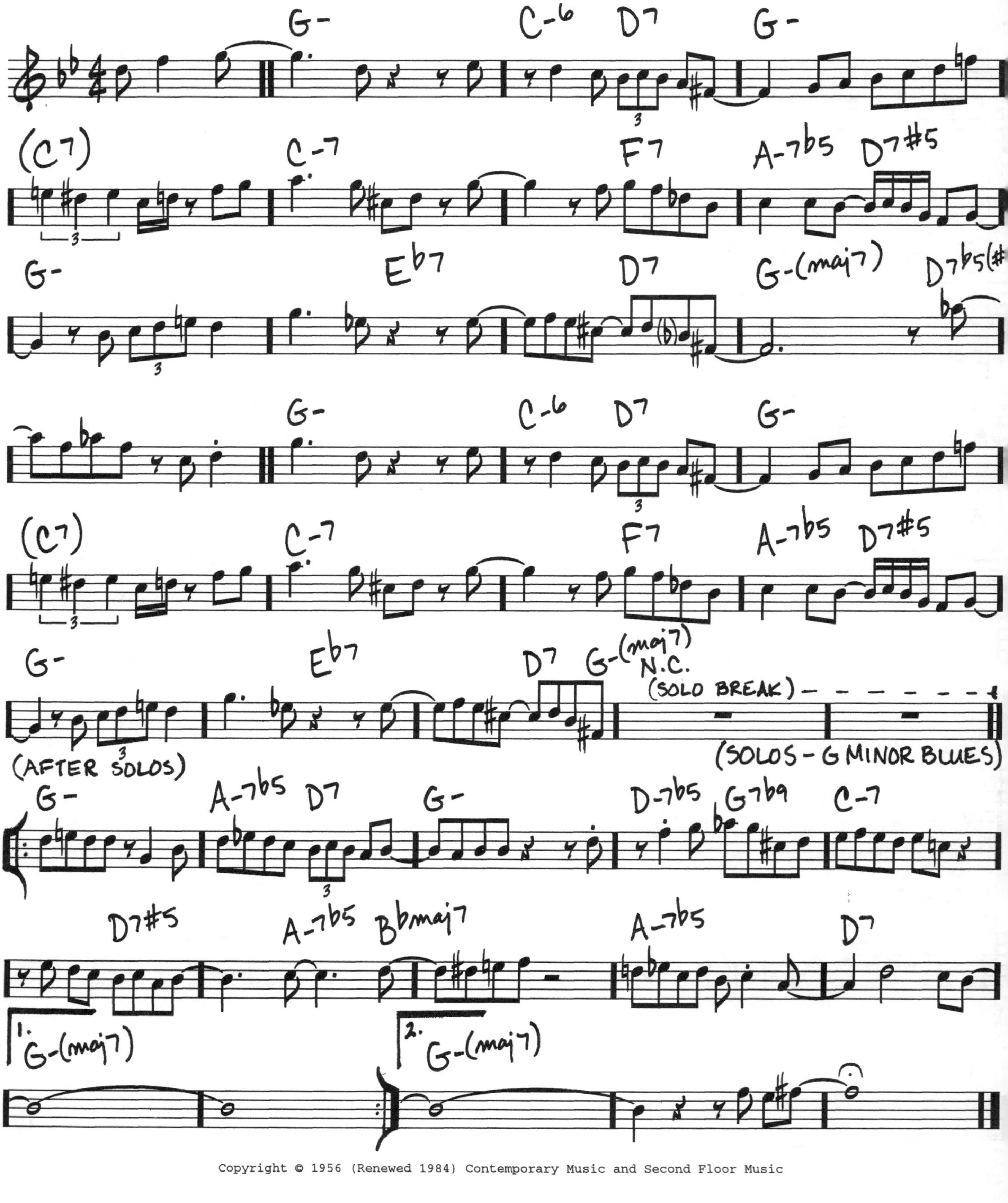

THEME FROM MR. BROADWAY

(UP)

-Dave Brubeck

(ENDING)

REPEAT FOR SOLOS

MR. MAGIC

268
(MED. SLOW) FUNK

—Ralph MacDonald
William Salter

MONK'S MOOD

-THELONIOUS MONK

(BALLAD)

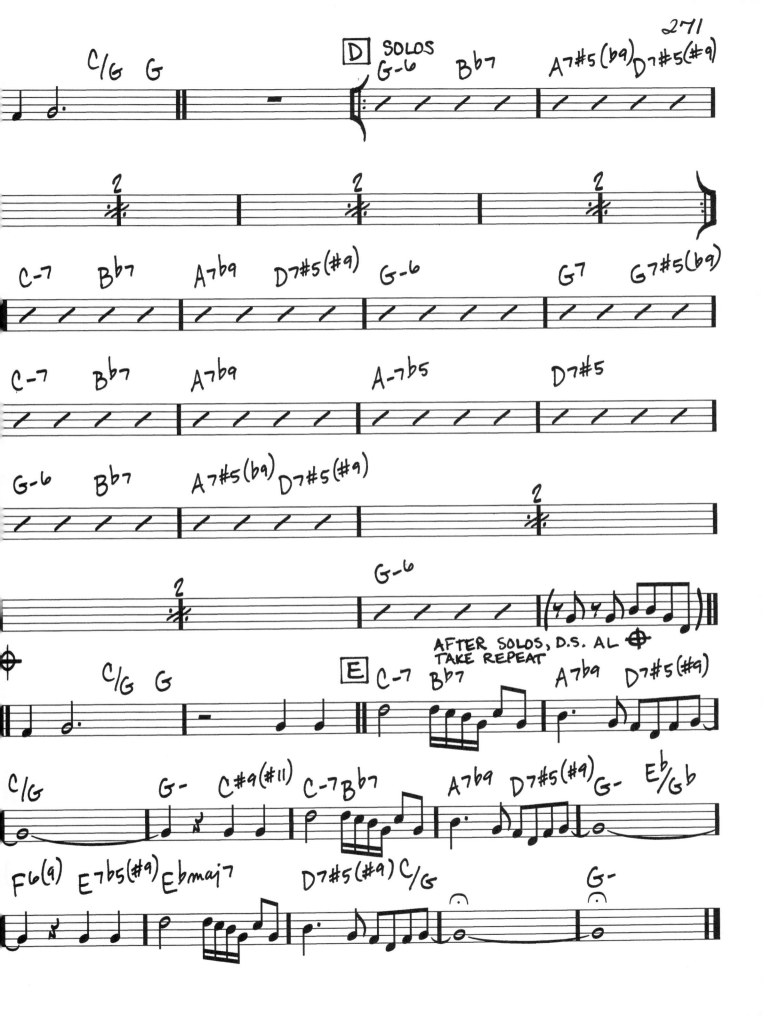

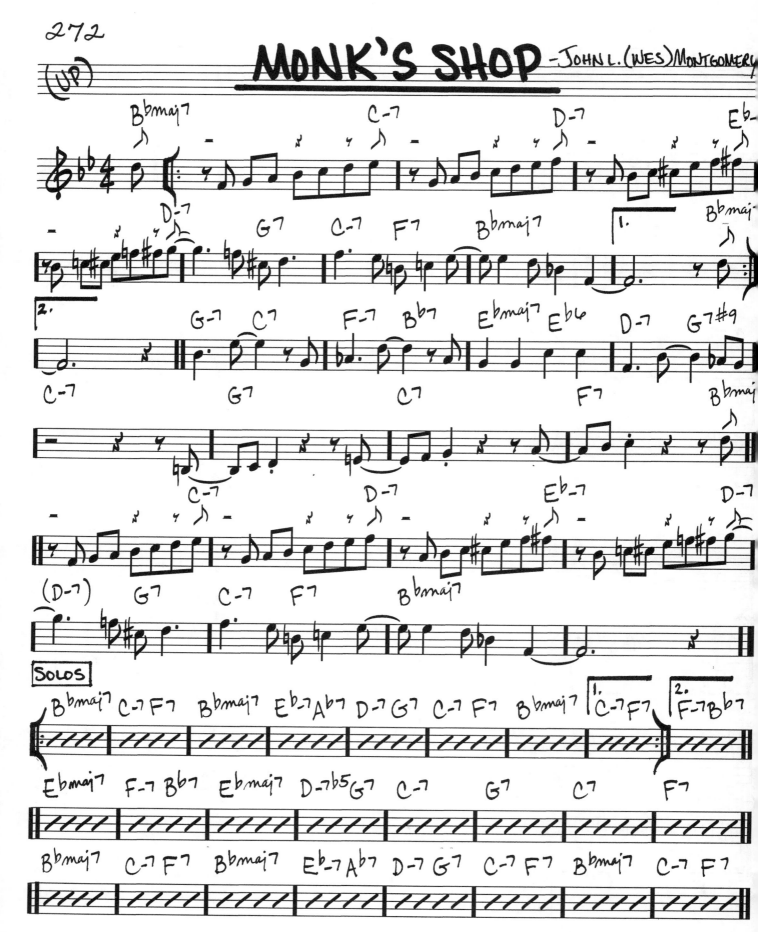

274
(BALLAD)

MOON RIVER

-Henry Mancini/
Johnny Mercer

MOONGLOW

275

(MED. BALLAD)

— Will Hudson/
Eddie DeLange/
Irving Mills

(BOP)

MOOSE THE MOOCHE

-Charlie Parker

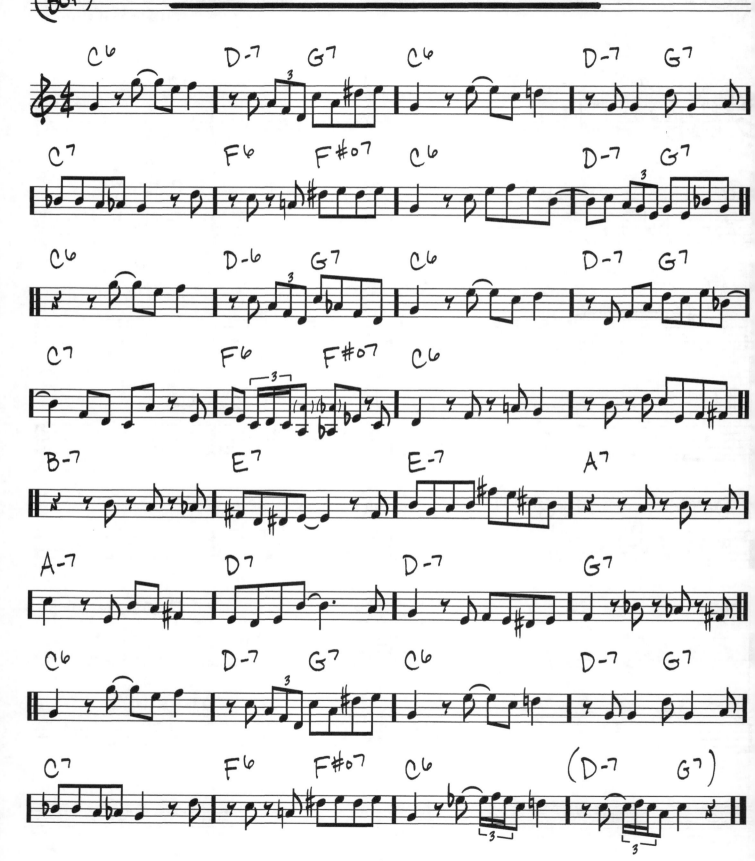

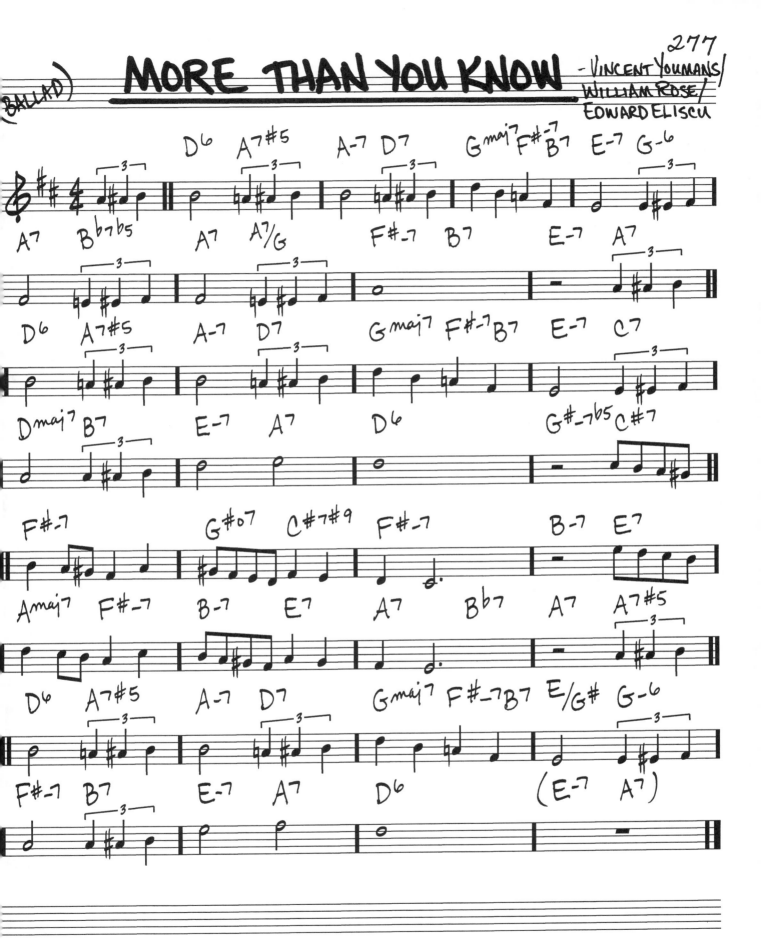

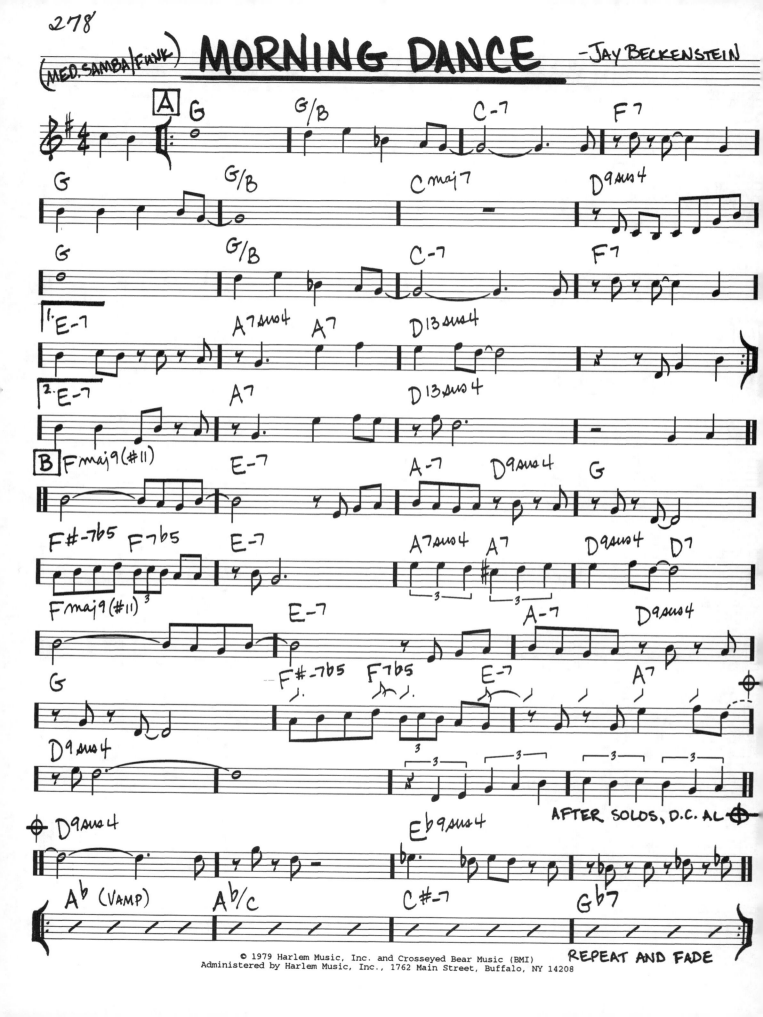

Moten Swing

—Buster Moten/ Bennie Moten

(UP)

Move

-Denzil De Costa Best

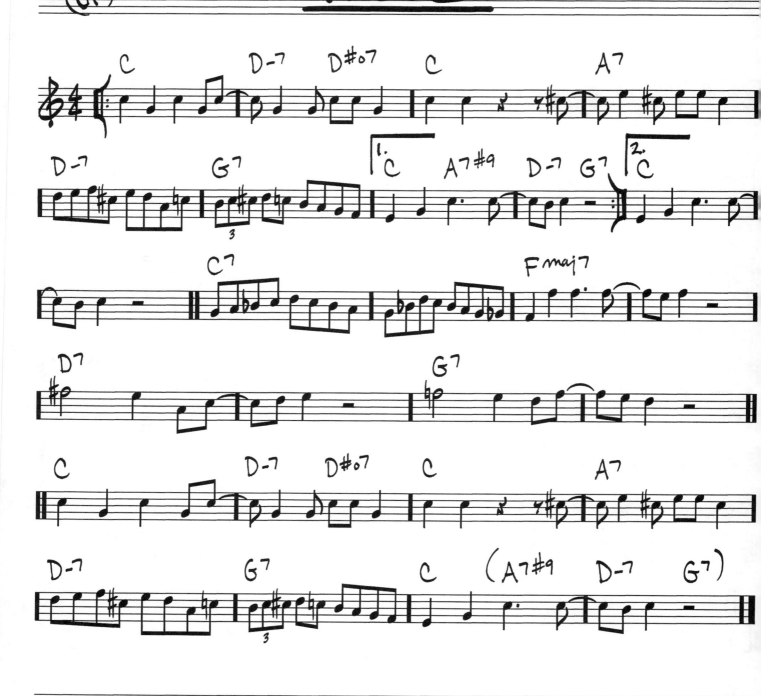

MY ATTORNEY BERNIE

(MED. SAMBA)

—DAVE FRISHBERG

AFTER SOLOS, D.S. AL ⊕

MY OLD FLAME

— Arthur Johnston /
Sam Coslow

(Ballad)

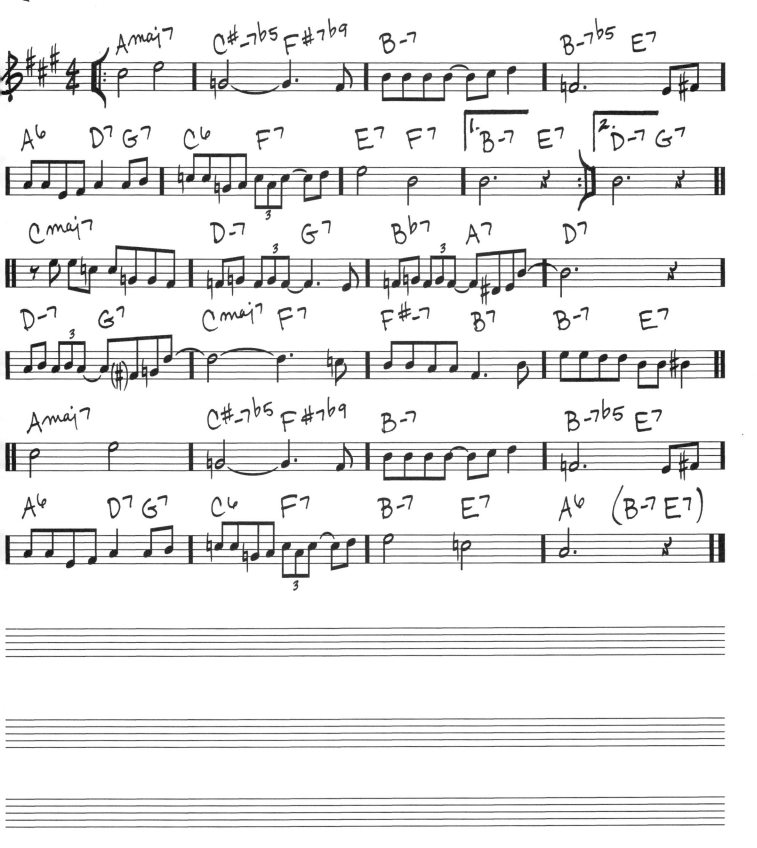

NATURE BOY

284
(BALLAD
(EVEN 8ths)

— Eden Ahbez

RIT. (LAST x) – – – 1

THE NEARNESS OF YOU

(Ballad)

— Hoagy Carmichael/Ned Washington

No Moe — Sonny Rollins

NO SPLICE

-Lee Konitz

(MED. UP)

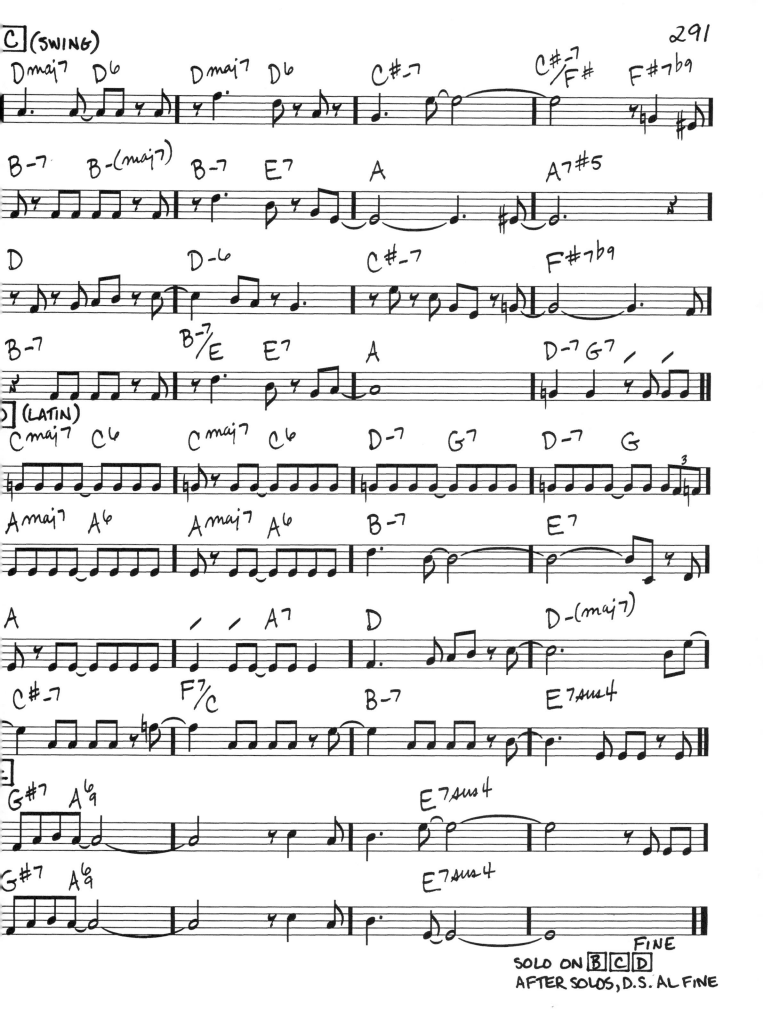

292

Now's The Time

-Charlie Parker

(Fast Blues)

REPEAT HEAD IN/OUT
AFTER SOLOS, D.C. AL ⊕

OFF MINOR

-Thelonious Monk

(MED. SWING)

OH, WHAT A BEAUTIFUL MORNIN'

(MED.-FAST WALTZ)

-Richard Rodgers/Oscar Hammerstein II

OLD DEVIL MOON

(MED.) — Burton Lane/ E. Y. Harburg

(SWING) ON THE SUNNY SIDE OF THE STREET

-Jimmy McHugh/Dorothy Fields

300
(MED. SWING)
ONE FOOT IN THE GUTTER
-CLARK TERRY

Our Language Of Love

302

(MED. FAST)

ONE MORNING IN MAY
—Hoagy Carmichael
Mitchell Parish

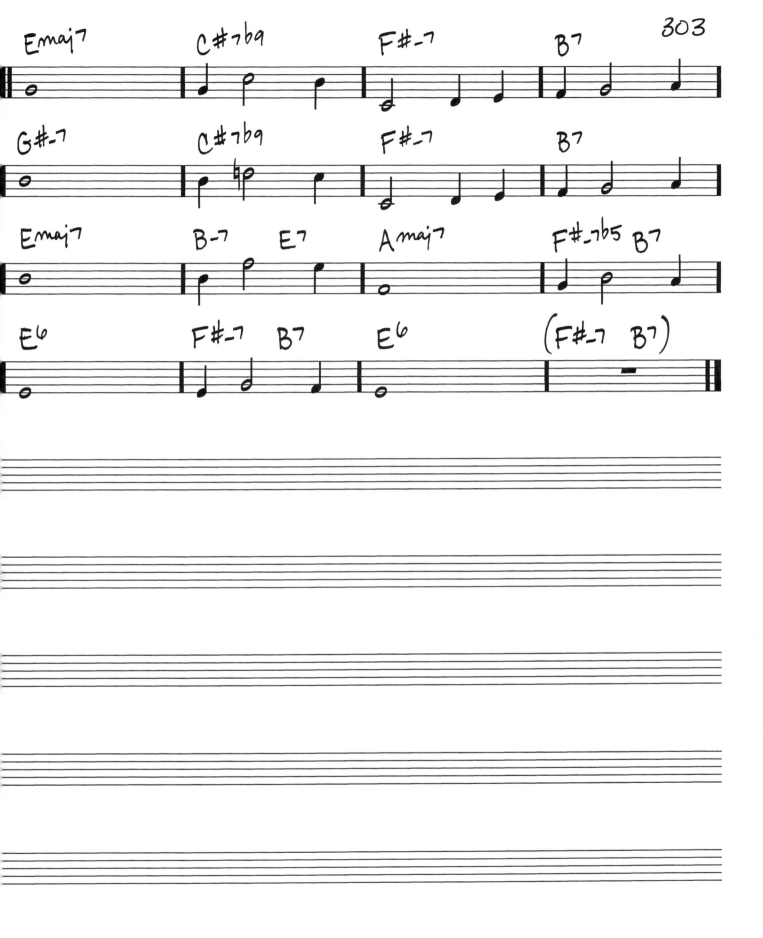

304

OUT BACK OF THE BARN
(SLOW SWING) —GERRY MULLIGAN

OYE COMO VA

—TITO PUENTE

(MED. LATIN)

After solos, D.S. al ⊕ (Take Repeat)

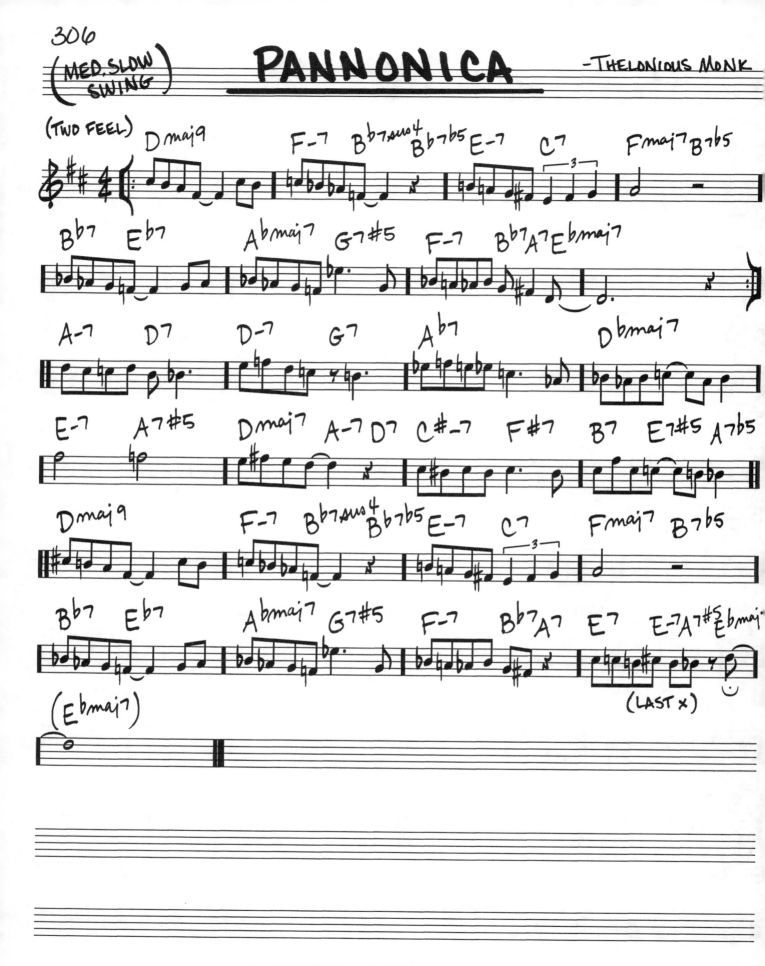

PARISIAN THOROUGHFARE

(UP)

-EARL "BUD" POWELL

PEEL ME A GRAPE

(MED. SLOW)

-Dave Frishberg

PENNIES FROM HEAVEN

(MED.)

-Arthur Johnston/
John Burke

310

PEOPLE WILL SAY WE'RE IN LOVE

(MED. SWING)

-Richard Rodgers/Oscar Hammerstein II

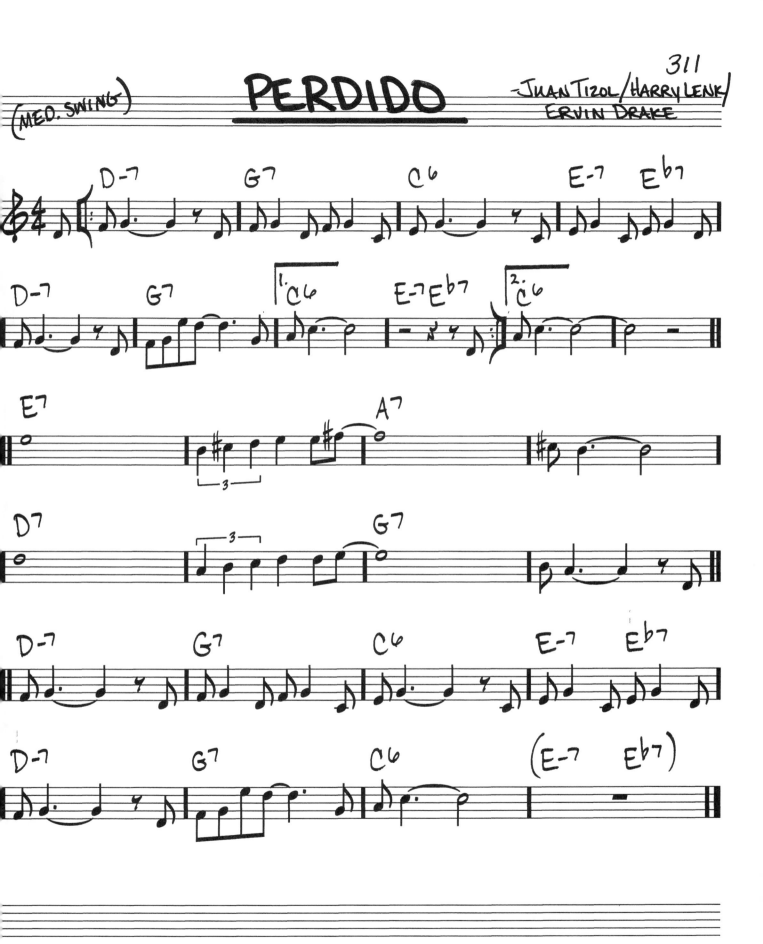

PHASE DANCE

— Pat Metheny / Lyle Mays

314

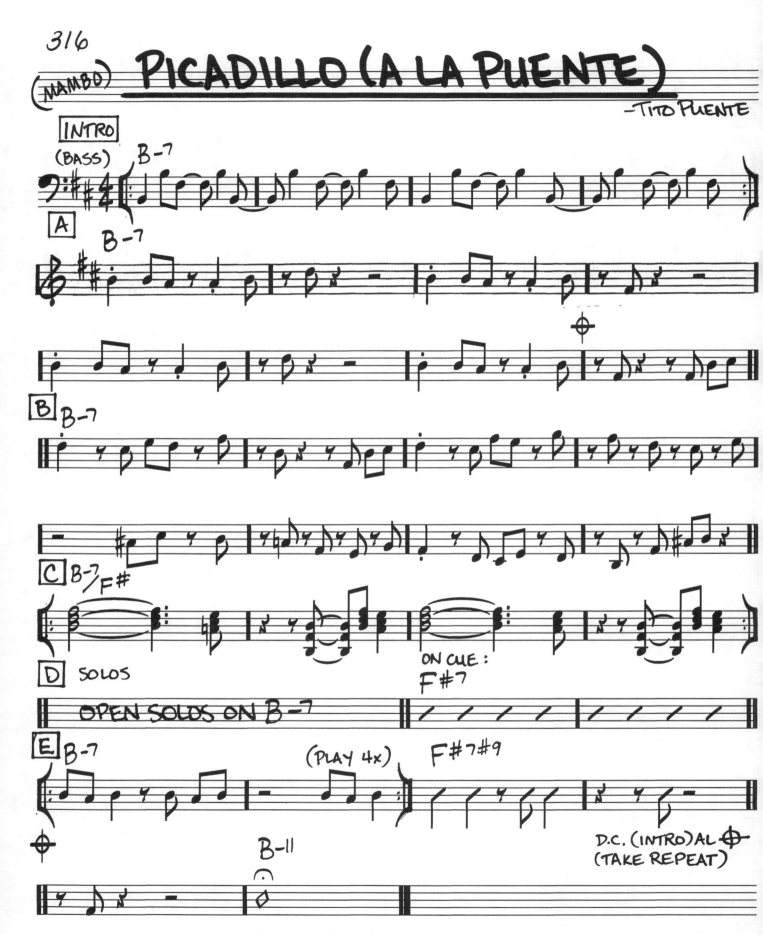

PICK YOURSELF UP

(MED. UP) — Jerome Kern / Dorothy Fields

317

318

POLKA DOTS AND MOONBEAMS

A PORTRAIT OF JENNY

(Ballad)

-Gordon Burdge/J. Russell Robinson

PRISONER OF LOVE

(MED.)

— Leo Robin / Clarence Gaskill / Russ Columbo

Pursuance
(PART III)
-John Coltrane

322

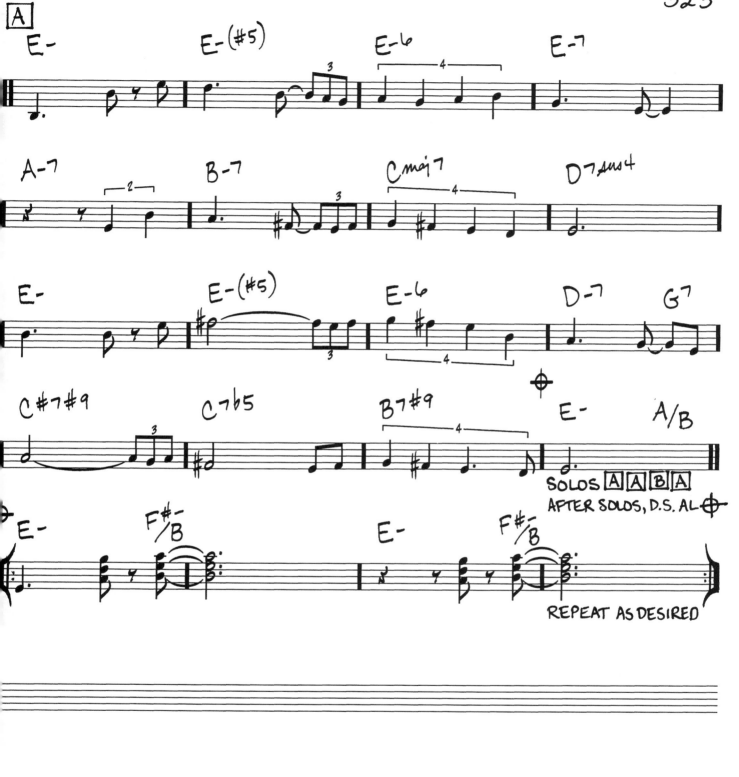

RAN KAN KAN

—Tito Puente

RED CROSS

(BOP)

– CHARLIE PARKER

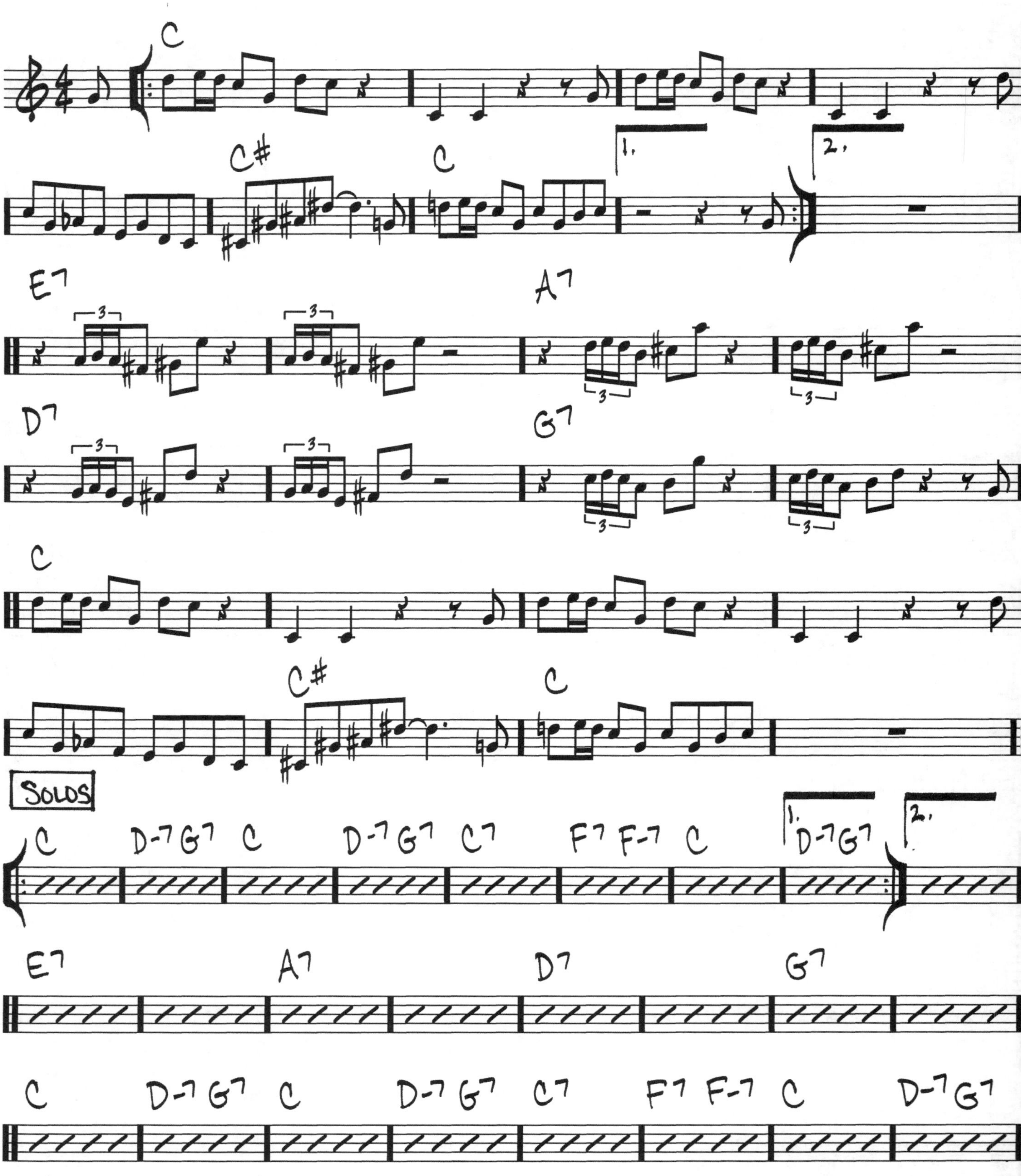

THE RED ONE

—PAT METHENY

(FAST REGGAE) EVEN 8THS

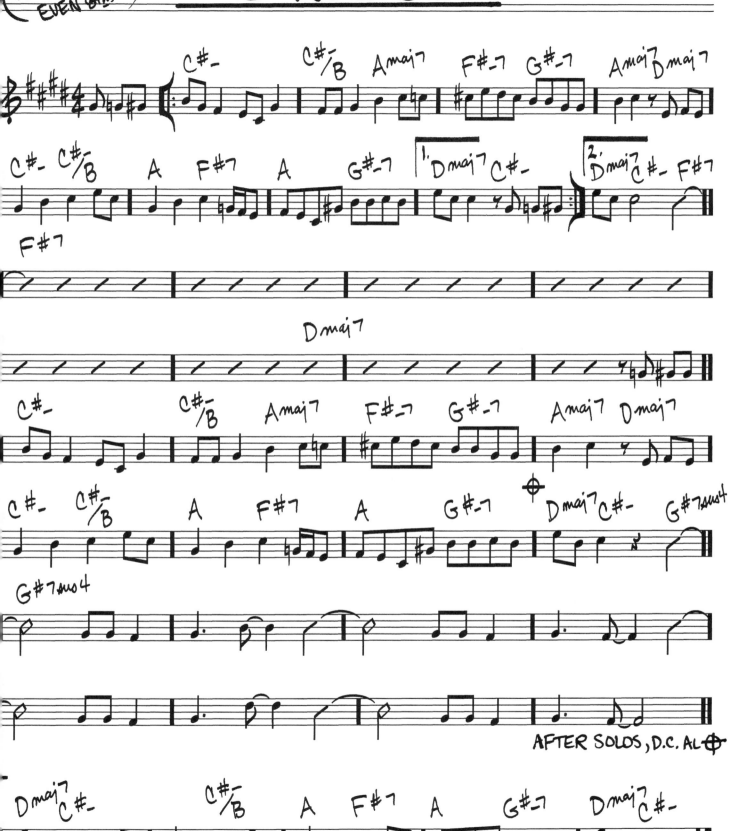

AFTER SOLOS, D.C. AL ⊕

Right As Rain

(Ballad)

Harold Arlen / E.Y. Harburg

330

ROBBIN'S NEST

(MED. SWING)

—Sir Charles Thompson
"Illinois" Jacquet

ROUND TRIP

— Ornette Coleman

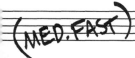

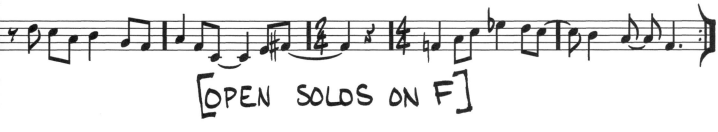

[OPEN SOLOS ON F]

ROUTE 66
— Bobby Troup

SACK OF WOE

—Julian Adderley

338

ST. THOMAS

-Sonny Rollins

(CALYPSO)

REPEAT HEAD IN/OUT

SANDU

-CLIFFORD BROWN

SENTIMENTAL JOURNEY

(MED.)

-BUD GREEN/LES BROWN/BEN HOMER

SERENADE TO A SOUL SISTER

JAZZ (WALTZ)

-Horace Silver

SHUTTERBUG

-J.J. Johnson

SILVER'S SERENADE

(MED.)

— Horace Silver

SIPPIN' AT BELLS

-Miles Davis

(MED. BOP)

352

SKYLINER

—Charlie Barnet

(BRIGHT SWING)

[SOLO ON ENTIRE FORM]

SMOKE GETS IN YOUR EYES

-Jerome Kern
Otto Harbach

(Ballad)

ALSO PLAYED & BOSSA - DOUBLE RHYTHM VALUES

Softly As In A Morning Sunrise

355

— Sigmund Romberg / Oscar Hammerstein II

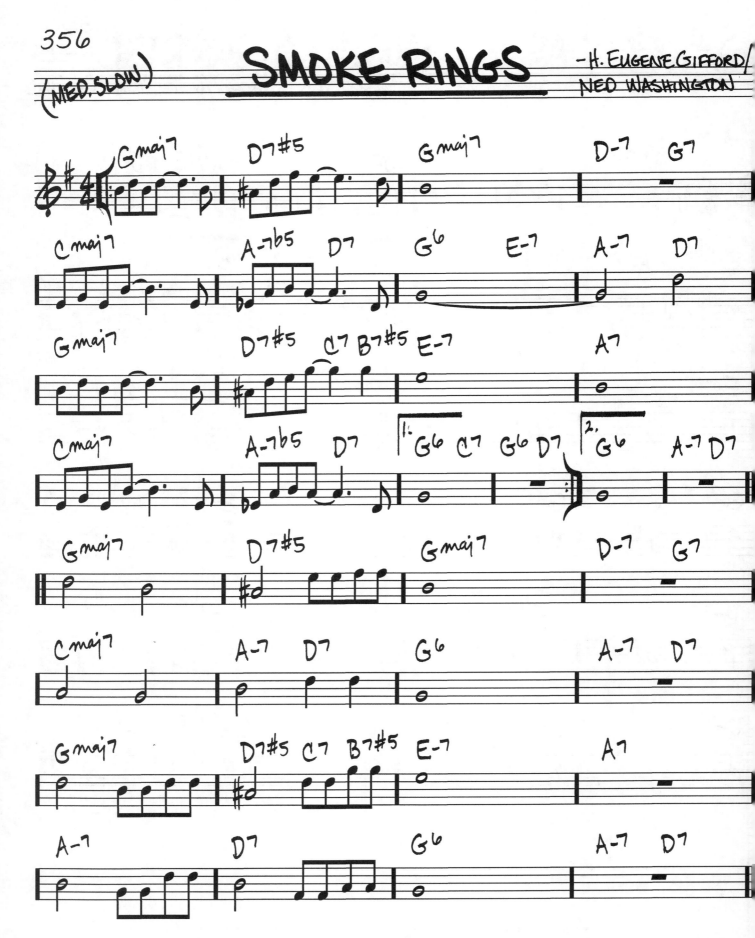

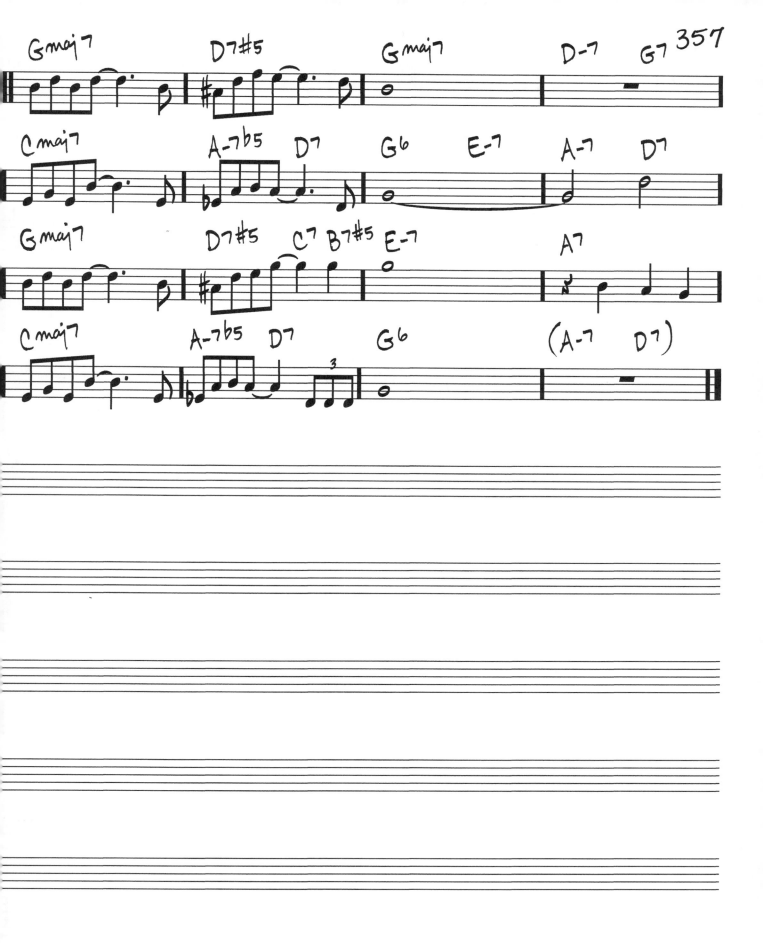

SOME OTHER BLUES

—John Coltrane

SONG FOR BILBAO

— Pat Metheny

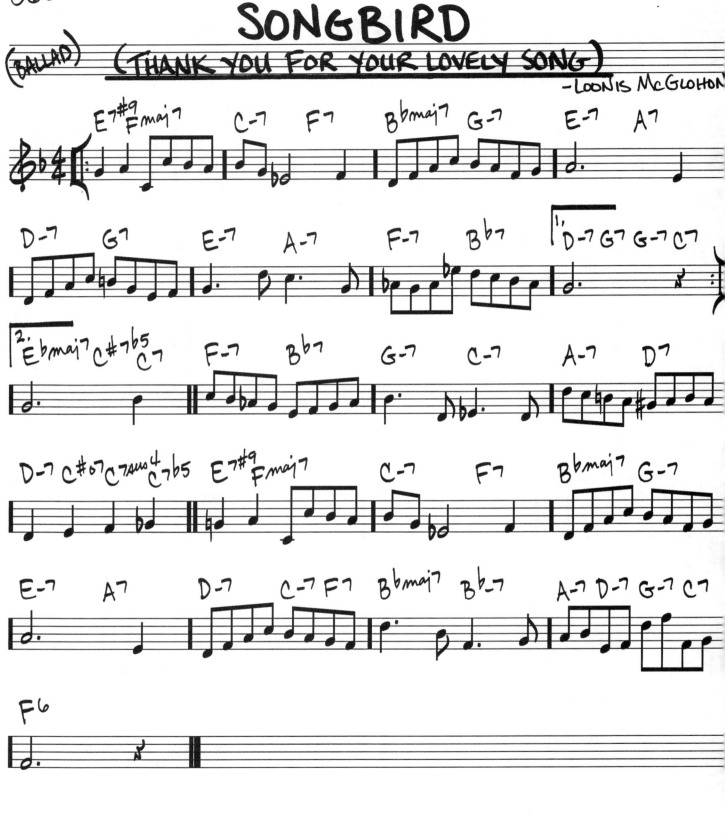

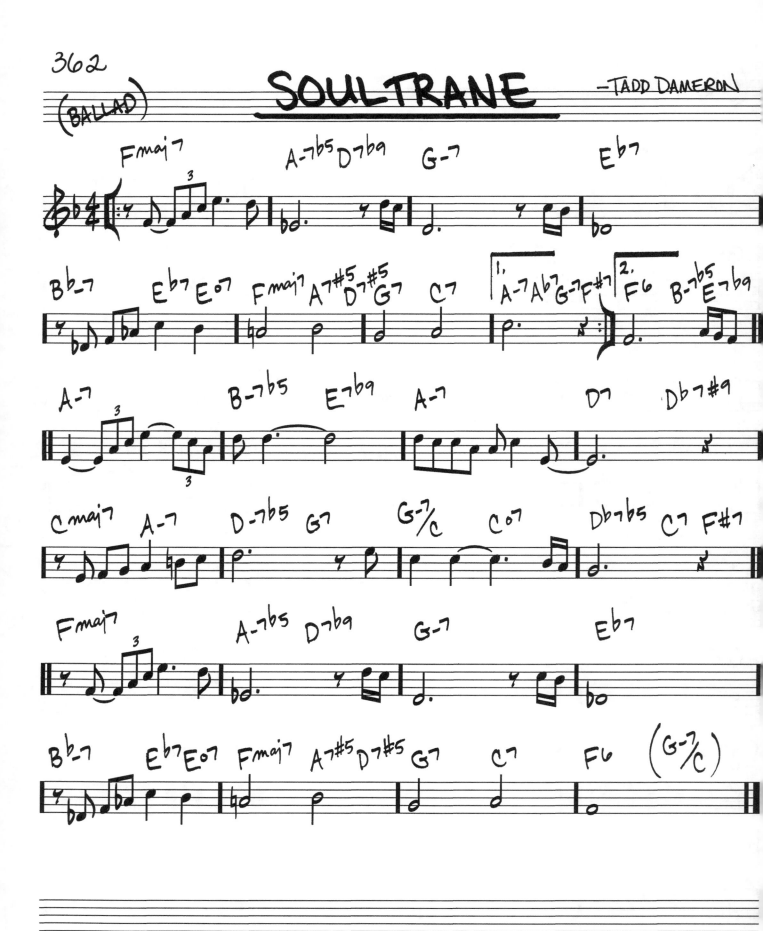

362

SPEAK LIKE A CHILD

(MED. LATIN) — Herbie Hancock

SOLO

VAMP

AFTER SOLOS, D.C. (TAKE REPEAT)
FADE OUT OVER VAMP

SPEAK LOW

-Kurt Weill/
Ogden Nash

(MED.)

SPIRAL

—John Coltrane

(MED.)

ST. LOUIS BLUES

—W.C. Handy

[SOLO ON A BLUES]

STARDUST

Hoagy Carmichael / Mitchell Parish

(MED. BALLAD)

STRAYHORN 2

— GERRY MULLIGAN

(BALLAD)

STROLLIN'

— Horace Silver

BASS WALKS ON SOLOS
AFTER SOLOS, D.C. AL ⊕
(TAKE REPEAT)

373

SUBCONSCIOUS LEE

—LEE KONITZ

(MED. UP)

REPEAT FOR SOLOS
AFTER SOLOS, D.C. AL ⊕

374

376

378

THE SWEETEST SOUNDS
(MED. FAST)
— RICHARD RODGERS

THE SWINGIN' SHEPHERD BLUES

— Moe Koffman/Rhoda Roberts/Kenny Jacobson

[SOLOS ON C BLUES]

'Tain't What You Do
(It's The Way That Cha Do It)

-Sy Oliver/
James Young

(MED.)

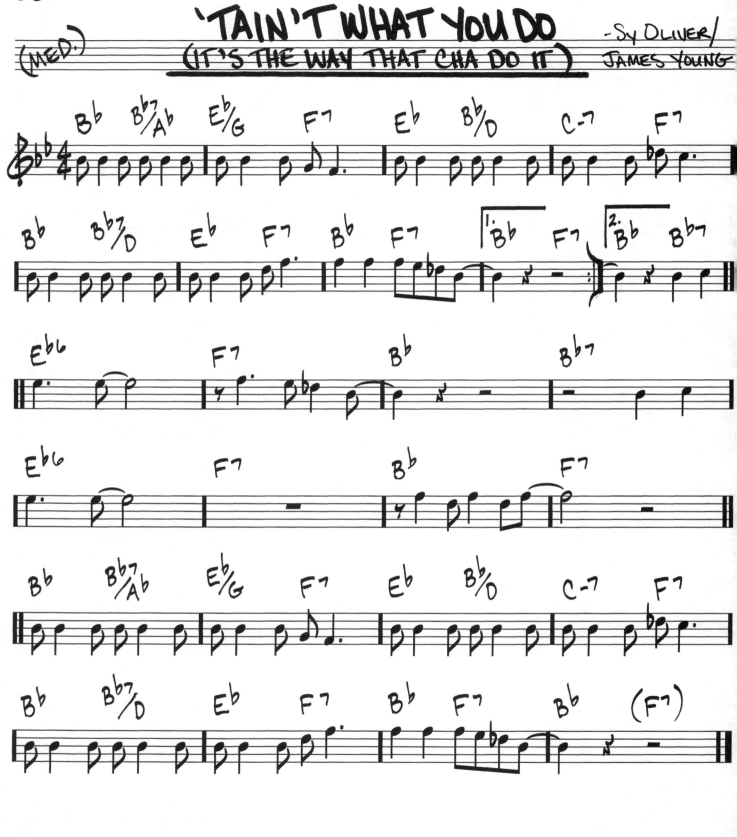

TAKE THE COLTRANE

-Duke Ellington

(UP)

384

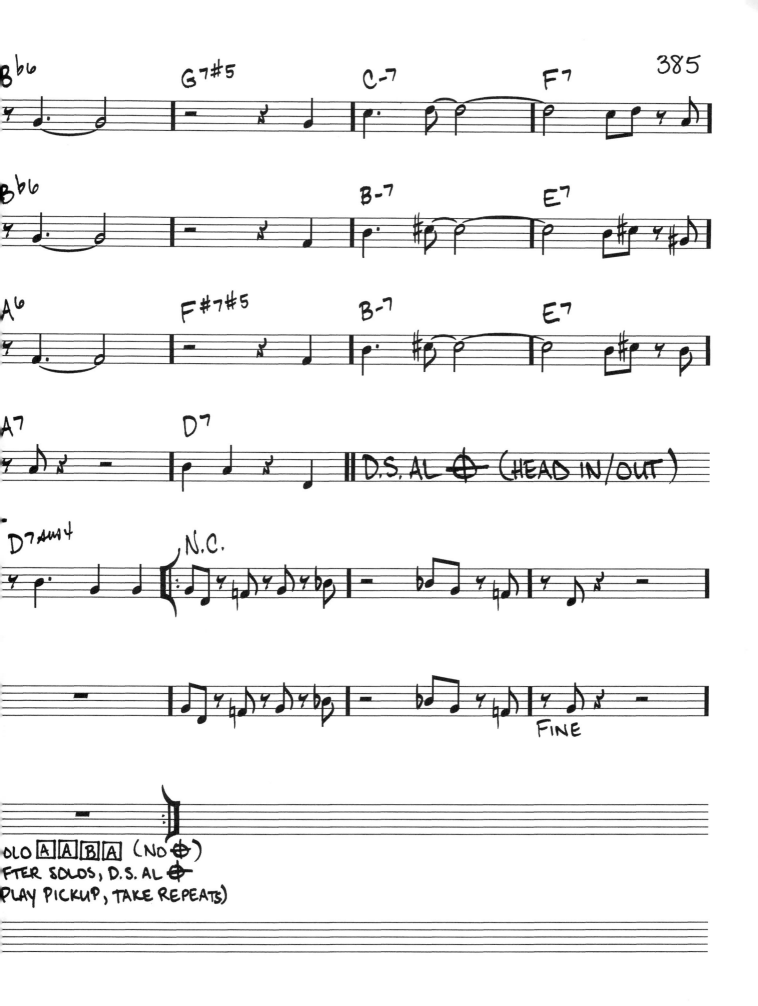

TEMPUS FUGIT

— Earl Bud Powell

(Fast Bop)

Tenderly

—Walter Gross/ Jack Lawrence

(MED. BALLAD)

TENOR MADNESS

(MED. UP)

— Sonny Rollins

THERE'S A SMALL HOTEL

(MED.)

-Richard Rodgers / Lorenz Hart

392

THINGS TO COME

(UP)

—Dizzy Gillespie/ Gil Fuller

(BALLAD) THE THINGS WE DID LAST SUMMER

-JULE STYNE / SAMMY CAHN

THIS I DIG OF YOU

— HANK MOBLEY

[SOLO ON C BLUES]

THIS YEAR'S KISSES — Irving Berlin

(BALLAD OR MED.)

© 1950, 1957 (Renewed) FRANK MUSIC CORP. and MEREDITH WILLSON MUSIC

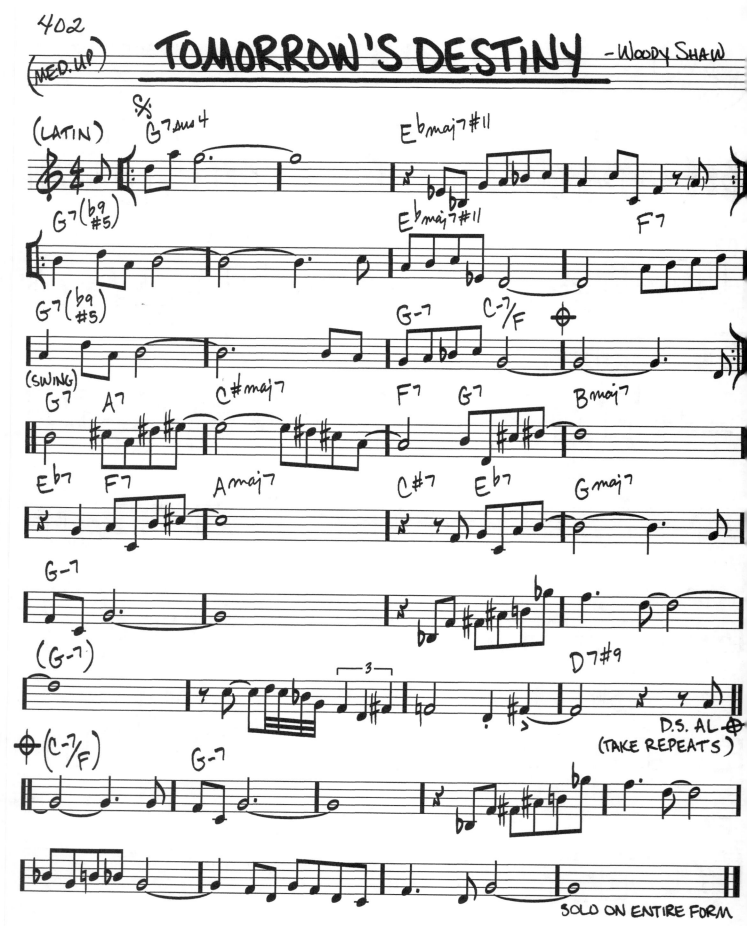

SOLO ON ENTIRE FORM

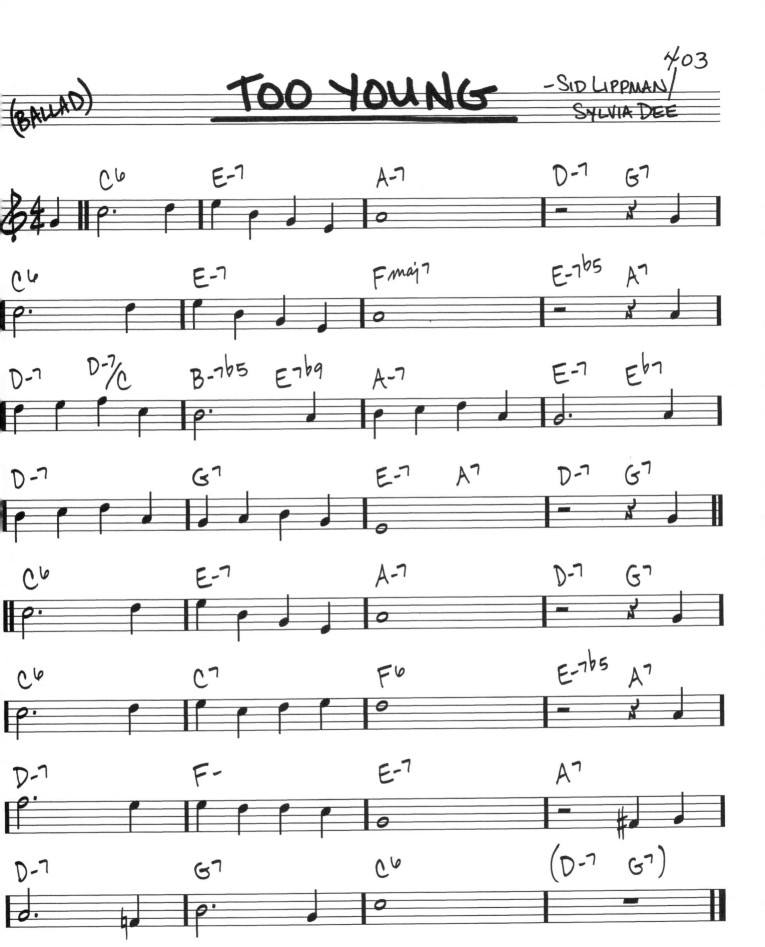

Too Young

(Ballad)

—Sid Lippman / Sylvia Dee

403

404

(MED. BLUES)

TRANE'S BLUES

—John Coltrane

[SOLOS ON D BLUES]

406
(MED.)

TWISTED

—WARDELL GRAY

(MED.) TWO CIGARETTES IN THE DARK

— LEW POLLACK / PAUL FRANCIS WEBSTER

408

(MED. BLUES) TWO DEGREES EAST, THREE DEGREES WEST

-John Lewis

UNTIL I MET YOU
(CORNER POCKET)

(MED. SWING)

— Freddie Green/ Don Wolf

409

410

A WALKIN' THING

411

-Benny Carter

(MED.)

412

WARM VALLEY

(MED. BALLAD)

— Duke Ellington

Watch What Happens

(Bossa)

— Michel Legrand/Jacques Demy/Norman Gimbel

The Way You Look Tonight
(Slow)

-Jerome Kern/Dorothy Fields

415

A WEAVER OF DREAMS

416
(MED. OR BALLAD)

—Victor Young
Jack Elliott

418

WENDY

—Paul Desmond

(MED. SLOW)

© 1975 (Renewed) Desmond Music Company

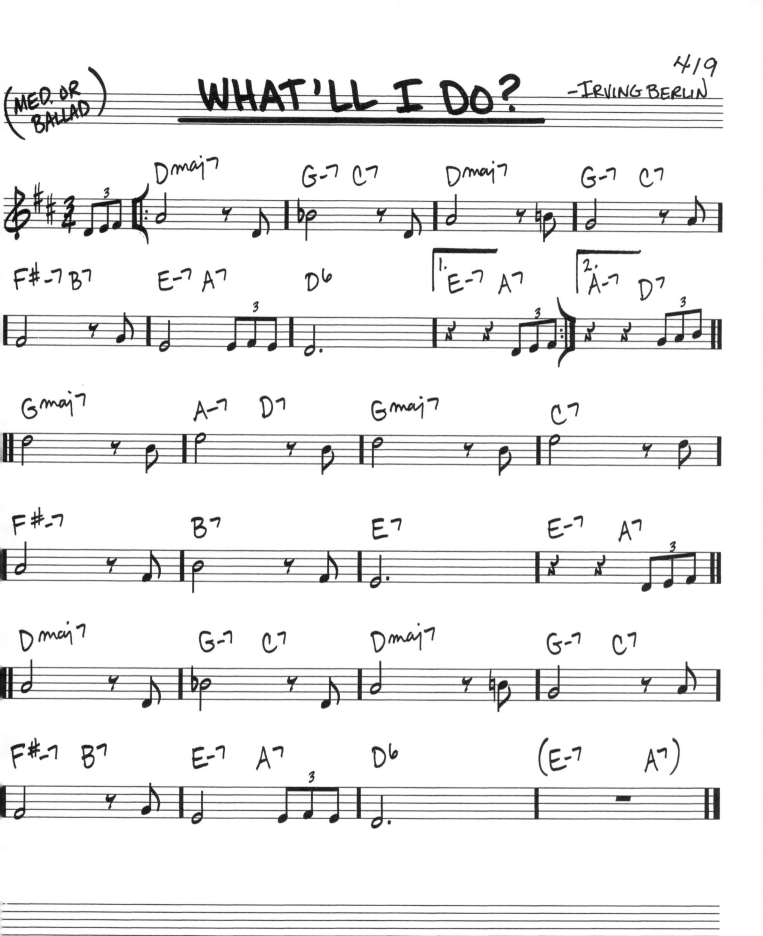

WHEN LIGHTS ARE LOW

(MED.)

– Benny Carter / Spencer Williams

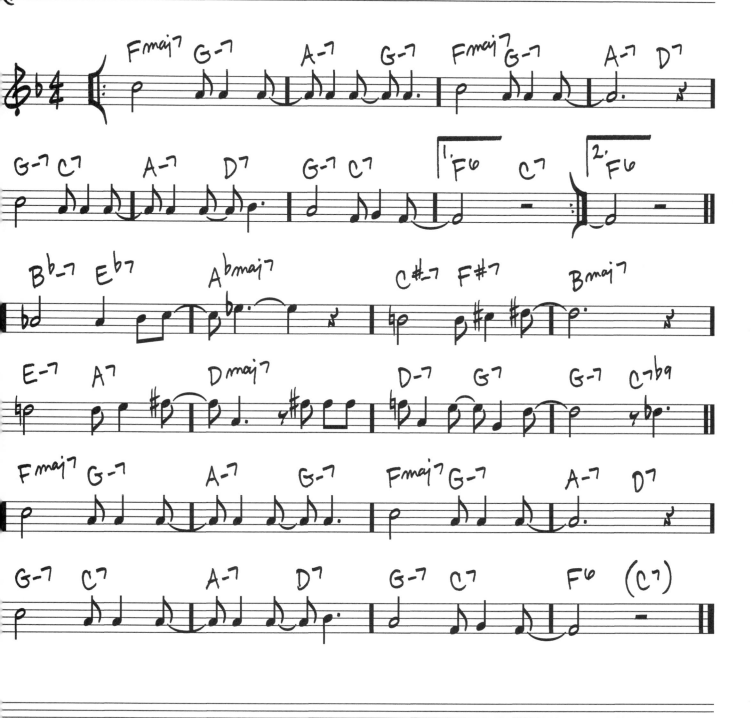

WHISPER NOT

— Benny Golson

(MED.)

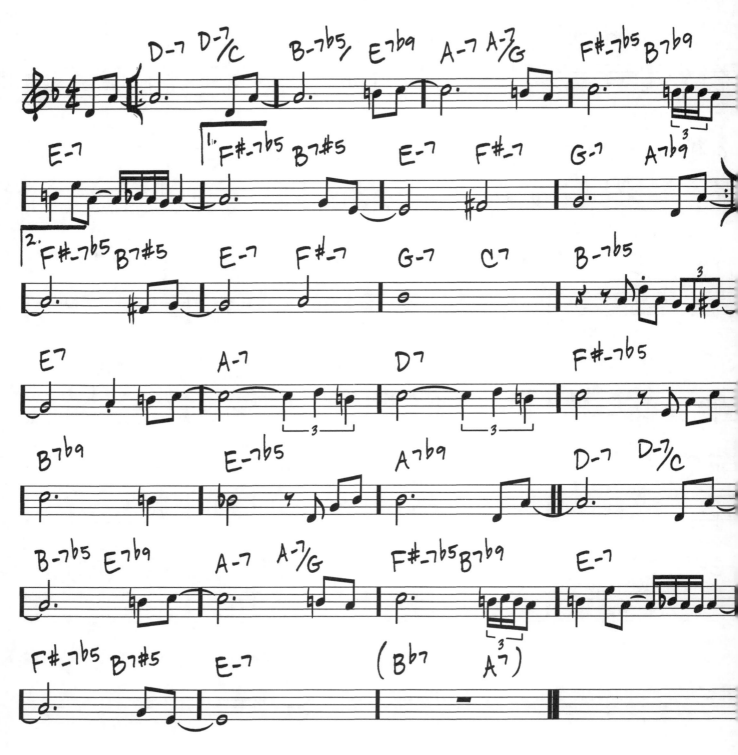

WHO CAN I TURN TO
(WHEN NOBODY NEEDS ME)
- Leslie Bricusse / Anthony Newley

(MED. BALLAD)

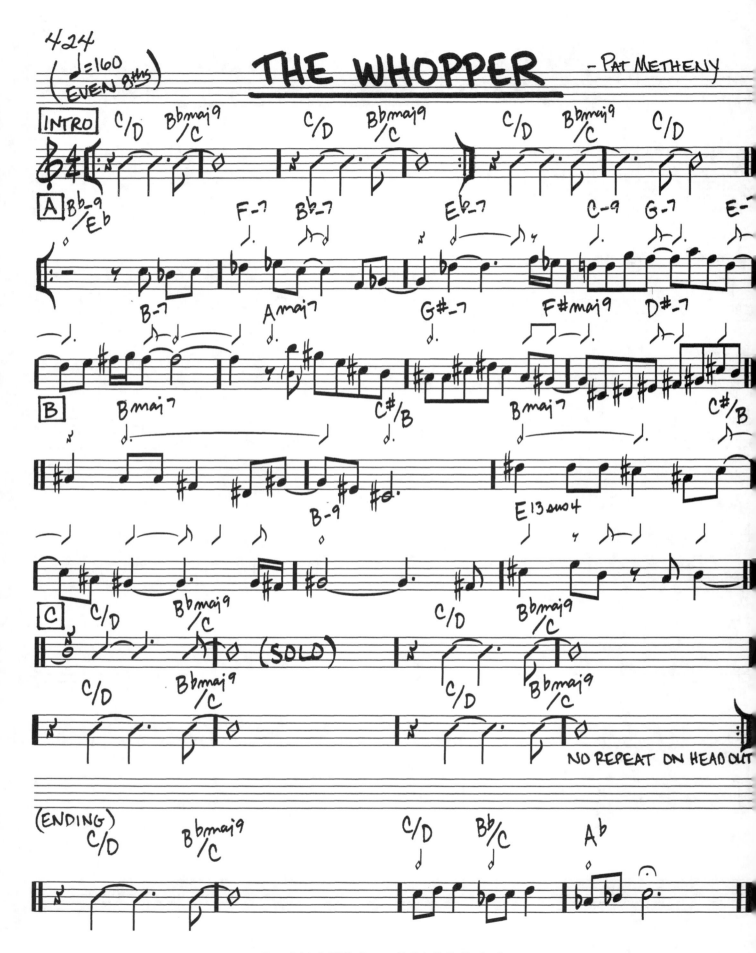

WHY DO I LOVE YOU?

—JEROME KERN/OSCAR HAMMERSTEIN II

(MED.)

WORK SONG

— Nat Adderly/
Oscar Brown, Jr.

(MED.)

430

(BRIGHT) A WONDERFUL DAY LIKE TODAY

-Leslie Bricusse/Anthony Newley

YARDBIRD SUITE
— CHARLIE PARKER

(MED. UP)

AFTER SOLOS, D.C. AL ⊕
(TAKE REPEAT)

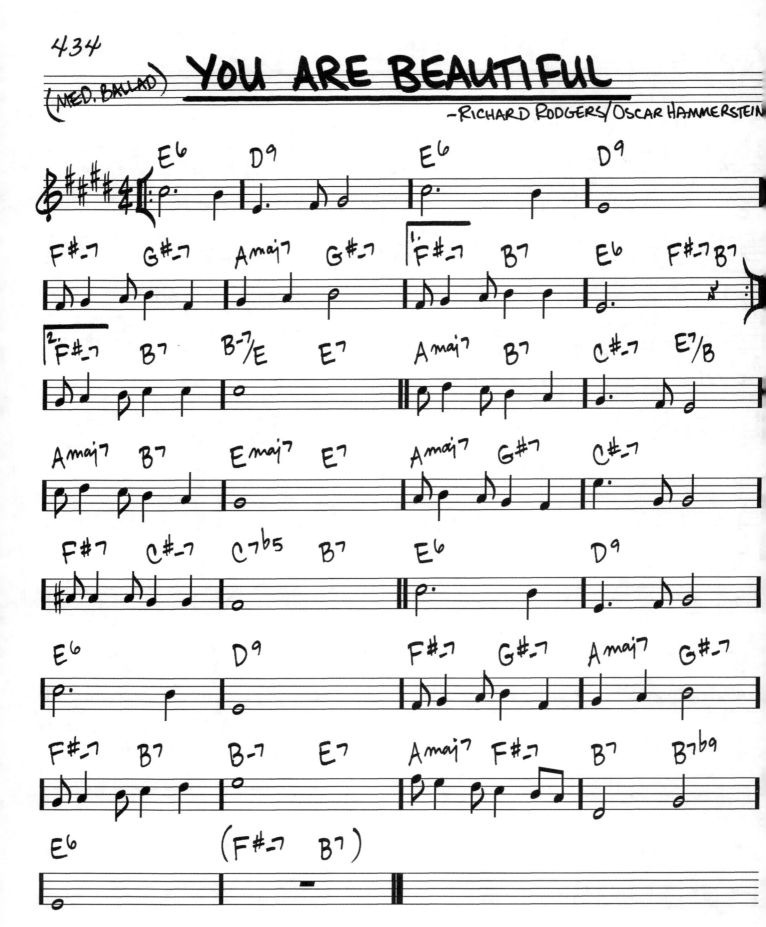

434

(MED. BALLAD) YOU ARE BEAUTIFUL

-Richard Rodgers/Oscar Hammerstein

You Can Depend on Me

-Charles Carpenter / Louis Dunlap / Earl Hines

(Med. Fast)

436
(MED.) YOU'D BE SO NICE TO COME HOME TO

- Cole Porter

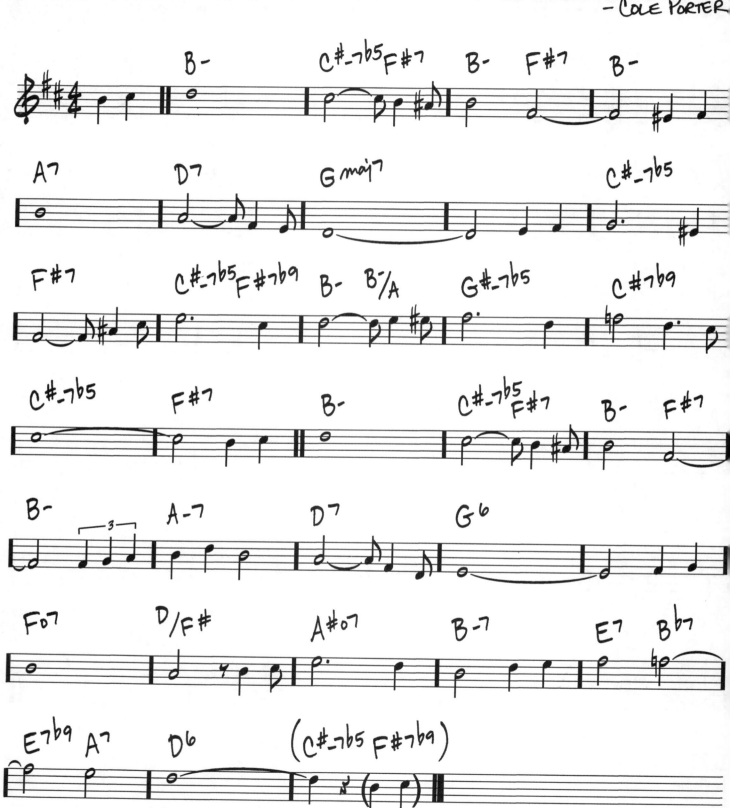

You're My Everything

— Harry Warren/Mort Dixon/Joe Young

(Med.) You're Nobody 'Til Somebody Loves You

-Russ Morgan/Larry Stock/James Cavanaug

REAL BOOKS AVAILABLE

C, B♭, E♭ & Bass Clef Editions for:

The Real Book – Sixth Edition, Volume 1

The Real Book – Volume 2

The Real Book – Volume 3

More editions coming soon.

See your music dealer to order.

7777 W. BLUEMOUND RD. P.O. BOX 13819 MILWAUKEE, WI 53213

Visit Hal Leonard Online at
www.halleonard.com